Rogue Patrol

by

Ray Palmer

Copyright © 2025 Ray Palmer

ISBN: 978-1-918038-56-9

All rights reserved, including the right to reproduce this book, or portions thereof in any form. No part of this text may be reproduced, transmitted, downloaded, decompiled, reverse engineered, or stored, in any form or introduced into any information storage and retrieval system, in any form or by any means, whether electronic or mechanical without the express written permission of the author.

Foreword

It has been quite a long time ago now, but back in the summer of 1971, I was a Parachute Regiment soldier serving in Belfast.

I had left my hometown of Wolverhampton, in the West Midlands in 1968, aged just 15, and now, my new home consisted of barracks in Aldershot.

In 1969, the unrest in Northern Ireland had prompted the government to send troops there. It was only a matter of time that I would be sent there, but first, I had a 12 month course in London to attend.

Belfast '71: I was one of the youngest soldiers in the unit, and after my constant grumbling of being stuck inside, my superiors finally agreed that I could go out on an evening patrol.

I was fed up of being cooped up in the mill (our lovely accommodation) and missing out on all the action, but the boss had my best interest at heart as I was the youngest, although I didn't agree with him.

Finally, on my very first patrol after about an hour just off the Falls Road, a shot was fired by the patrol commander. He gave a warning before he fired, and the round never hit the commander's target. That was the baptism of my first patrol, and now many years later that true incident has now inspired me to write the following story.

I pondered on a 'What if'... What if a patrol made a serious error? ... What could happen if it was covered up? ... And what would happen when the police discover a body years later?

The story 'Rogue Patrol' reflects such a scenario, resulting in a can of worms being opened of huge proportions and someone is trying to put a lid on it; suppressing it at all costs.

The investigation spreads further afield, when the police in the UK mainland are dragged into it, culminating it into a dramatic conclusion. Full of twists and turns, I hope you the reader, will enjoy my mystery thriller.

I would like to acknowledge the following for the help they have given me in writing my novel.

Maureen Harrison,
Georgina Garbett,
John Donnelly,
Dee Palmer (former member of Jethro Tull)

Northern Ireland 9th July 2002

Detective Sergeant Pat Connelly adjusted the aircon as he made his way down the A1 from Belfast.
The July sun was now burning through the windscreen.
"Why is it always bloody hot when I am at work, and never when I'm home with the kids?" he muttered.
Pat Connelly loved his job; he had joined the Royal Ulster Constabulary in 1985 after a short spell as a probation officer.
Pat was forty-two years old, married with two children. He enjoyed a decent pint of real ale and was more than happy to sit alone in a pub with a crossword puzzle and a pint.
The one problem Pat had, was trying to sleep when he was in the middle of an investigation, which sometimes made him cranky the following day.
In the passenger seat sat Detective Constable Mark Brookes, who was exploring the glove compartment.
"What you after?" asked Pat.
"Just wondering if there are any maps of Dromore, Sarge."
"The body has been found south of Dromore, so a map is unlikely to be much use, anyway, a local patrol car will flag us down, and guide us to the lake ... I hope.
Are you playing football tonight, Mark?

"Not at the moment, Sarge, some of the lads are on their hols, and Paul, who organises the games, will let me know when we can start, mind you I wouldn't really like to play in this heat to be honest."

"I don't blame you, Mark, it's a killer, isn't it?"

It wasn't long before they were south of Dromore, and DC Brookes gestured towards the parked police car. DS Connelly flashed his headlights and as per instructions followed the patrol car.

"DC Connelly and DC Brookes," announced Pat to the local police on the ground.

Sat down on the grass were four teenage boys, all looking very downcast and anxious. Four bikes piled on top of one another lay next to them.

"Which one of you found the body?" asked the DS.

"It was him, Mister!" two of the boys pointed to the boy wearing a Manchester United shirt.

The boys had clearly been swimming in the pool, why not, it was a hot day.

"I wanted to try out my snorkel and mask, see how deep the water is," exclaimed the boy. "What's your name, son?" asked the DC, who wanted to participate with the questioning.

"Michael ... Michael Cleary, Mister."

"Go on then, Michael, tell us what happened," said the DS egging him on impatiently.

"Go on, Mickey, tell him," said another boy, butting in.

"I made sure the mask was on with no leaks, then, swam down. The water suddenly became very cold, which I didn't expect, but I carried on.

I saw weeds at the bottom with a log, and what looked like a big bag next to it. I just pulled at what I thought was a bag and then saw it. A skeleton head with bits."

"Skull!" interrupted the DC.

"Jesus, it was terrible, the worst thing I've ever seen. I came straight back up."

"Then what, Michael?" asked the DS.

"Jimmy there," pointing in the direction of a smaller boy in a white T shirt, "He rode off to the main road and stopped a car and told the lady to get the police."

"DC Brookes, I want you to organise a local WPC to get the boys home, particularly Michael, as he's going to be having nightmares for quite a while after this, oh, and see if you can sort out some way of getting the bikes back, I've got to speak to the SOCO team."

"Won't that upset the Super, Sarge?"

"Hearts and minds, Mark, hearts and minds."

"If you say so, Sarge," replied the DC.

During the interview with the boys, frogmen brought the body up to the surface, without the attached log. It was placed to one side and cordoned off with tape, the same as used by the SOCO (Scene of Crimes Officer) team.

"Where is the SOCO team, they should have been here by now?" exclaimed the DS.

"Just arrived, Sarge, I can see them coming down the lane," replied a local PC.

The vehicle pulled up and 'The Prof' climbed out, immediately recognised by the DS. 'The Prof' was a character with a wicked sense of humour, in his sixties, and long greying hair, hence 'The Prof'.

"Bloody hell, if I had known you were here, I'd have brought a four pack, Pat, it's been ages since we had a beer."

"Nice to see you, Prof, hope you are okay as we have a strange one for you today, it scared the living daylights out of the lad that found him," said the DS with a wry smile.

"Well let's take a wee look, I've brought my knife and fork," joked the Prof.

"I'll be going back to base as soon as I've found my oppo. God knows where he's got to. Let me know ASAP, Prof, keeps my DI happy as he's an impatient sod."

3

"I'll do what I can, Pat, you know the score," replied the Prof.

Mark Brookes eventually caught up with his DS, who boasted that he managed to get the local garage owner to collect the boy's bikes."

"How much did you pay him?" asked the DS.

"Hearts and minds, Sarge, he jumped at the chance. Good publicity for him, isn't it?"

"Yep, hearts and minds yet again," replied the DS.

***

The following day, Pat Connelly finally got through to the Prof, after four attempts. "Well, I can tell you he was definitely shot ... through the chest and I would suggest an exit wound, but the body is badly decomposed," exclaimed the Prof.

"The round!" butted in the DS.

"No round I'm afraid, but I would say a high calibre weapon, maybe a 7.62 millimetre round caused the damage. Oh, and I can tell you he has been in that lake since 1971."

"1971!" answered the DS.

"Yes, found some coins that were decimal. Male in his thirties, maybe, early forties. Long hair and beard and a Timex watch was attached to his right wrist, which is unusual.

The other strange thing was, apart from money, nothing else showed up. No keys, papers nothing. We are in the process of dental records and DNA testing.

I will let you know if we get anything, Pat."

"Cheers, Prof, you're a star. We'll need a pic of the watch and full details. Now it's time for missing persons and the media circus. Here we go."

"Good luck, Pat," and the Prof signed off.

The Detective Inspector, James Walsh, had gathered everyone in the incident office the following day.

"Okay gents, and ladies," glancing over to his left, "I will be speaking to the coroner later, and I need as much info as possible. Pat, is there any more news from the SOCO team?"

"Not yet, Guv, I'm waiting for the dental reports still," replied a flustered Pat.

"Alright, this is a sensitive situation everyone. We are all aware that during the troubles people were abducted and never seen again. They have families out there, who are still desperate for information. So, when I eventually give out a press release, I want those phones manned, and full details taken of the callers, and gather as much information as you can ... with consideration. Also, don't forget the Timex watch. Now the body ... thoughts, Pat?"

"What comes to mind, sir, is an execution conducted by the Provos is usually a shot to the back of the head. They wouldn't normally go to all that trouble, to conceal a body. I mean, we don't up to now, know yet where he was killed. Another issue is the lack of belongings, and no ID and the way he was tethered to a log. His Parka jacket, which was full of stones, was used to tie his legs to the log and his belt tightened around his neck, also to the log.

To me, nothing was planned about this killing."

The DI remained silent. A raised arm caught the attention of the inspector. "D.C. Brookes."

"Could it be criminals, sir, maybe a fallout?"

"I doubt it, DC Brookes but thank you for your input. Right, everyone, we have work to do." DI Walsh hastily returned to his office.

DI Walsh was in his late fifties and mulling over his plans for retirement. He had served with the Royal Ulster Constabulary all his working life.

In 2001 the RUC was renamed the PSNI (Police Service of Northern Ireland). He had no doubts that DS Pat Connelly would be the right man to replace him, and that gave him some comfort, as he admired Pat for his tenacity and determination to solve cases.

In 1998, James Walsh, whilst painting his front window, fell from a ladder, and, despite an operation, still walked with a limp.

Whilst he wasn't officially deskbound, he was more than happy for Pat to do the legwork as walking and standing for too long made his leg ache.

On his office desk, amongst the clutter of phones and papers, lay a small pile of magazines that he had been reading. This was the evidence of his thoughts of retirement, a smart pile of organ magazines and brochures. 'At least it doesn't involve walking or standing,' he thought and smiled as he picked up his pipe and pouch of Clan, his favourite tobacco.

He filled his pipe, lit it with a match and sat down at his desk. When he was satisfied that the pipe was well lit, he picked up the top magazine and started to read it.

Wiltshire 1973

It was a pleasant evening in September, as the cars made their way along the driveway to the large house. One by one they pulled up in front of the large doors, and a hired footman walked smartly up to each vehicle and opened each door.

The ladies in long dresses, gentlemen in black tie attire and of course, officers of the regiment in mess dress.

At the door they walked through to the grand hall where they were met by Second Lieutenant Rory Furness. By his side stood his younger sister, Louise Furness.

Each of the guests were introduced to his sister. A waitress eagerly stood behind with a tray of glasses filled with sherry. As the guests arrived, there was the customary introductions as they mingled together for the next fifty minutes.

Ladies and Gentlemen! Will you please make your way to the dining room as dinner is about to be served," announced the servant.

The table is set for sixteen diners, with each place given a nameplate for each diner. Once the diners knew where their places were, they stood behind their designated chair.

A pianist continued to play at a grand piano in the corner of the room. Suddenly the music abruptly stopped as the doors swung open.

Brigadier Andrew Furness KBE accompanied by his wife Harriet, entered. The servant pulled out the chair for the Brigadier's wife. She gently sat down, and he likewise did the same for the Brigadier. Once sat down he gestured to all the guests to be seated. At that moment the pianist began to play Mozart's *Eine Kleine Nachtmusic*.

When the meal was well and truly over and the port was passed around, it was now time for the first toast. The Brigadier tapped the table with a small mallet and stood up.

"My, wife and I would like to welcome you all this evening. As you are all aware, it is in honour of my son, Rory's commission, and his first posting which is Northern Ireland of course.

I'm sure, along with myself, Harriet and Louise, that we all wish, Rory good luck and God speed. And above all, keep your bloody head down!"

That last sentence broke the ice with a few laughs and claps.

"Now, I am keeping with tradition as I make the first toast. Can you please be upstanding? Ladies and Gentlemen. Her Majesty the Queen." They all participated in the toast.

"And now Ladies and Gentlemen. Please raise your glasses to my son, Second Lieutenant, Rory Furness." All raised their glasses and drank the fine port, except Rory. He only reciprocated by raising his glass in appreciation, as he still harboured thoughts about his leadership.

'Was he truly, 'up to it?'

Northern Ireland 1973

The battalion were now eight weeks into a tour scheduled for two years. By now Lieutenant Furness had commanded several small patrols. The patrols were mounted in the countryside of Northern Ireland and generally could be uneventful.

On some occasions concentration could wane with thoughts of back home, favourite football team, TV programmes, food, alertness was paramount.

"Lieutenant Furness, sir, Major Gorman would like to see you in the office."

"Okay, Corporal, I'll be there in five minutes. Could you let him know please?"

"Sir," replied the Corporal saluting at the same time.

After about twenty minutes, the Lieutenant knocked on the door of the Major's office. "Come in please," a voice was heard from inside the room. "That's a funny five minutes, Lieutenant."

"Yes, sorry about that, the coffee was hot."

"Stand to attention, Lieutenant and what happened to the salute?"

"Sorry, sir."

"This is exactly why I've asked you here. I am your OC, responsible for all officers under my command. If I get it wrong, it's me that must face the music. You are too casual at times, Lieutenant. In the mess is one thing, where we can relax and chill out, but as soon as you walk out of the mess door in uniform, you become an officer in the British army. You cannot let your guard down. You're judged by your peers, your men and your enemies.

This is a friendly off the record chat, Lieutenant. I think you have everything it takes to become a good officer. Starting tomorrow, I want to see a difference in your approach. As for your platoon … don't be so familiar with them or you will regret it. A platoon commander earns the respect of the men. If you give an order, it must be obeyed immediately, not questioned back by the men in your platoon. Have you got my drift?"

"Yes, sir. I'm sorry if I have let you down. It won't happen again; you can be sure of that, sir." The lieutenant saluted smartly this time and marched out of the office.

Lt Rory Furness gathered his platoon together for a briefing. "Okay, gents, five man patrols this evening. Sergeant Strong, you take privates, Williams, Buchanan, Sorbie and Taylor.

Corporal Greenwood, you will have, Dickson, Groves, Angel and Hurt. Quiet! ..." he bellowed. The young lieutenant wasn't to be taken lightly, not after being chastised earlier in the day.

He had plans, the army was his future, and he wanted to prove to his father that he could match him. His father, now a Brigadier, had made his name fighting in the Korean war, where he was mentioned in dispatches.

"Lastly, Lance Corporal Sanderson, Astley, Wilkins, and, Stevens, you're with me. Wilkins you have only been in the platoon five minutes, so stick with Corporal Sanderson, and do what he says, understand?"

"Yes," came a feeble reply.

"Yes, Sir and stand to attention," shouted the lieutenant, "didn't they teach you anything at depot?" he continued.

"Sorry, sir," said Wilkins, on this occasion firmly standing to attention.

"How you got through P company is a mystery to me, Wilkins." Groves, under his breath, whispered to Angel, "He thinks he's the fuckin' RSM all of a sudden."

"The rest of you are not required this evening. Sergeant Strong, fall the men out."

"Yes, sir," replied Sgt Strong, who continued to finish his instructions, "and if you think you're playing on the pinball game in the canteen all afternoon, think again, 'cos the block needs cleaning, it's in a shit state. Those of you on patrol … outside the guardroom, 16:00hrs. I'll be checking weapons," continued the Sergeant. "Officer on parade, FALL OUT!" he bellowed.

The platoon, did a right turn, smartly saluted, and marched off the square. Lieutenant Furness returned a casual salute as he walked away.

P company, was the Parachute Regiment's physical training course at Aldershot, considered by many to be the toughest military course in the world, apart from some special forces such as the SAS (Special Air Service) and SBS (Special Boat Service).

If the military personal made it through P company, (many didn't) then they could move forward to the actual parachute training school with the RAF. Those who completed their parachute course, would then be awarded their wings.

L/Cpl Lennie Sanderson was the joker of the platoon, a natural leader and a bit of a 'Jack the lad'. His hometown was Farnborough, about 3 miles away from his barracks in Aldershot, also nicknamed 'The Shot' by local soldiers. Lennie was appointed second in command of the patrol that evening.

From the West Midlands, Private Derrick Astley was the quiet one, he never questioned an order, and was very competent with all his military skills, but unlike the others of the patrol he had no interest in sports and struggled with his physical fitness.

Private Jack 'Stevo' Stevens was from Lancashire. The others in the platoon took him for a Mancunian due to his strong accent, which did make him sound like a Manchester lad. He always corrected them with "Burnley ... best place in the world."

Like Lennie, Stevens was a bit of a joker but with a darker side, particularly with the new boy Wilkins, who was easy pickings for Stevens. More than once, Lennie had told Stevo to lay off taking the mickey out of Wilkins constantly.

Pte Russell 'Wilco' Wilkins was a West Country lad, at only 19 the youngest soldier in the platoon. His mistakes made him a target for Stevens, as well as jibes from his platoon commander Lt Furness and Sgt Strong. At least he found comfort that Lennie Sanderson was trying at helping him fit in, as well as help from Derrick Astley.

The battalion were stationed in proper brick-built barracks, as opposed to factory buildings, warehouses and mills. These were used for short tours, usually four months.

Weapons generally consisted of the SLR (self-loading rifle). Ammunition consisted of a magazine using 7.62mm (millimetre) calibre rounds that packed a deadly punch. A weapon that was particularly popular amongst British paratroopers.

The Stirling SMG (Sub machine gun), a small weapon that used 9mm ammunition, was noted for clearing buildings and not accurate unlike the SLR.

Then there was the heavy GPMG (General purpose machine gun), belt fed, once again with 7.62mm ammunition.

Lieutenant Furness had made the decision for his patrol to all use the SLR. The patrol was later dropped off by a long-based Land Rover south of Dromore, with an arranged collection at 07:00hrs the next day.

The area was mainly open fields, copse, hedgerows, small woods and a small lake. The patrol, after a few checks eventually walked away slowly keeping well apart. Daylight was expected to last up to 19:30hrs.

At 22:15hrs they trundled in the darkness along a hedgerow. In front, the lieutenant who was leading the patrol could make out the dark shapes of a wooded area. He studied the area in a dreamlike state thinking of home, and the MG sports car in the garage waiting for his attention.

Just out of the blue, the movement of a shadow moved up taking the shape of a figure. Without any hesitation, he cocked the weapon with his left hand and with his right thumb pressed down the safety catch, aimed the SLR and fired once.

The figure in front slumped to the ground as the large crack of the sound of the rifle filled the air.

The soldiers in the patrol had already hit the ground. Corporal Sanderson came up to the kneeling position as the lieutenant slowly walked forward, still pointing the SLR in front.

Looking ahead, with his left hand, beckoned the others to move forward. "Come on," Corporal Sanderson whispered to the others.

By now, lieutenant Furness was standing by the body of this bearded scruffy man lying there, eyes wide open. "What just happened?" asked the Corporal.

"I saw him going for what looked like a gun, there must be a handgun here somewhere," exclaimed the lieutenant.

By now the rest of the patrol had joined the two. "Shit, I've never seen a dead person before," said a voice at the back.

"Get your torches and find the gun. Best start there, and slowly come forward in a row," suggested Corporal Sanderson, pointing at a spot about two yards in front of the body, "and do not touch it if you find it."

After fifty minutes had passed, the patrol had turned every bit of grass and shrub over on their knees. All the time the officer never said a word. "Can't find it, sir. We've looked all over; did you actually see it, sir?" asked Pte Steven's.

"I'm sure it was a gun he had. I had to move quickly, didn't I?"

"Corp, why are his trousers down?" asked Astley, who had been studying the corpse intently. "Christ, he was having a shit," said Stevens.

The moment of terror had now hit Lieutenant Furness as everyone in the patrol looked at him. He had killed a man who was having a crap, nothing more.

"What's going to happen now, sir?" said an inquisitive Stevens.

The legs of the Lieutenant were buckling underneath him. It was like a bad dream, but he wasn't going to wake up from this mess. His career was over, and he knew it.

There are four witnesses, unless … "Okay, guys, gather round. What I am going to say now stays with us and no one else, including the rest of the platoon. Do I have your agreement, all of you, yes or no? go ahead, talk between yourselves."

"I don't really understand what you mean, sir," said a confused Stevens.

"I'll put it like this. Suppose he was a Provo, and did have a gun. It was dark and I saw him before you guys did. He would have likely taken at least two of you out, especially at this close range. I had to make a decision in a milli-second, which would have saved your lives.

Instead, we have a dead vagrant by the looks of him. So can I speak to you, off the record with a proposition?"

They were intrigued by what their officer had got to say, not so much Wilkins who was way out of his depth with the whole incident.

Finally, they agreed to hear this proposition. "Remember, you all agree that the proposition I'll put to you now, is between us and no one else. Let me hear each one of you swear by it." Each one took it in turns, even Wilkins.

"Okay then, I intend to stay in the army, it's my life, some of you guys might opt out for civvy street. My career is finished if this gets out ... £10,000 for each of you tomorrow, if you all forget about it. That will give you a great start in civvy street and enough to buy out if you want to." There was a stunning silence. "It was me who shot him, not you guys. Just keep quiet and its £10,000 for each of you."

"How are you going to get the money, sir?" asked Stevens showing an interest.

"I'll get as much cash as I can tomorrow from Downpatrick and arrange to collect more over the next week or two. Also, I will go easier on the four of you, not the rest of the platoon. That will be a relief to, Private Wilkins." The latter statement brought a small laugh, breaking the ice a bit.

"It's best that I put in a transfer to another unit, or the others might smell a rat with me going easy on you four. I'll make up some excuse and then you will see the last of me."

"What about him?" Corporal Sanderson said, pointing at the corpse.

"Leave that to me, but I will need a volunteer if one of you can give me a hand ... okay chaps ... it's 'make your mind up time', as they say on Opportunity Knocks."

The men of the patrol were still very quiet. It was a lot to take in. "Well, I'm up for it, ten thousand smackaroos. I'm out in twelve months' time and I fancy running my own pub and that will do it." Corporal Sanderson announced. Surprisingly Wilkins chipped in with, "Me too, the army's not really for me, and the money would be useful." The pressure was suddenly on Stevens and Astley.

"Why not, but I might stay in the regiment so nobody better squawk," explained Stevens. All eyes are now on Astley. "I didn't sign up for this," Astley protested.

Lieutenant Furness watched the proceedings in silence. This was his only chance, now resting on Astley, who was wobbling. Should he intervene or let it play out? Patience, let it play out, let them grind Astley down.

"Astley," suddenly the lieutenant intervened, "what if you have been taken ill and your involvement in this never happened. Of course, there wouldn't be any £10,000 but the rest of us would keep mum, and you have played no part in it, and taking money would make you part of it. Your amount would be divided up between the other three. Also, don't forget that you have sworn to secrecy our conversation?"

"How does that work with the illness?" piped up the Corporal.

"Simple, we move a few clicks away from here and radio for an ambulance. Meet up on the main road and wait for the meat wagon. All Astley must do is groan a lot and keep his hands on his stomach.

We get back on patrol till we get picked up in the morning. No one heard the shot as we are in the middle of nowhere, and who's gonna miss an old tramp? Its Astley's choice, and if he wants to wave away ten grand, let him decide."

Once again there was silence. Checkmate thought Rory Furness, now feeling a little more confident of the outcome.

Astley finally announced his intentions. "Okay, I'll be ill, I don't want to be involved, sorry. I will keep quiet as this never happened as far as I am concerned. On paper the shooting happened after I was taken ill to hospital. That's what you mean, sir isn't it?"

"Exactly, Astley," replied the lieutenant.

"You had better stick to it, or you'll be looking over your shoulder for the rest of your life, won't he, sir?" piped up Stevens.

"I am sure Astley will keep his silence. At the end of the day, he's still one of us, a Para … am I correct, Astley?"

"To right, sir."

"As I said before, I will ease off you guys and that includes Astley. You all okay with that … good? Right guys, have a good look around for stones, as many as you can find and bring them here, we need to put a bit of weight on our man here."

The four of them went off in different directions with torches shining towards the ground. After a few minutes Wilkins shouted out to the others that he had struck gold.

It wasn't long before the officer was kneeling on the ground, stuffing all the jacket pockets on the body with rocks and stones. Some stones were even stuffed up the jacket as tight as possible. "Now I need a volunteer with some muscle." Stevens's hand rose into the air. "Well done, Stevens, come with me."

The two of them walked off into the distance then returned shortly after, with Stevens now soaking wet without his smock (Parachute regiment military jacket) and shirt. "Never volunteer in the army. I should have known better," exclaimed Stevens.

The officer put his arms underneath the arms of the body, whilst Stevens grabbed the legs, and both shuffled off into the trees.

They had found the perfect place to dump the body, and Stevens had to make sure it was deep enough.

After about five minutes a noise was heard by the others. They turned towards the sound of the splash.

They watched in silence, then gathered themselves together and sauntered off by the tree line. "Time for you to earn a fuckin' Oscar now, Astley," said a drenched Stevens who was in the process of changing back into uniform. It was followed by a few chortles as they finally made their way to the main road.

All of what the patrol had just done since the weapon was fired, had been heard and observed for the last two hours.

Watched by a pair of eyes within the woods that they had just left. The eyes belonged to a man with long hair and a dishevelled beard, wearing an old Parka jacket, dirty denims and muddy boots. Next to him lay a rucksack that had seen better days.

His name was Rab Anderson.

***

Three days later back at the barracks Lt Furness had arranged for the platoon, under the instruction of Sgt Strong, to do some drill practice on the square. But just before the platoon marched away the Lieutenant instructed L/Cpl Sanderson, Privates Stevens and Wilkins to fall out and wait there. Sgt Strong then marched the platoon to the square.

"Alright, now the coast is clear make your way to your billets, quickly," instructed the Lieutenant. The three of them arrived in Pte Stevens room. Each room had four beds. Stevens sat on his bed the other two sat on another bed in the room while they waited for the officer.

"I wonder why Astley isn't here?" asked Wilkins, with cigarette smoke coming out of his mouth.

"We'll soon find out; I can hear footsteps coming. I bet it's the boss," said Sanderson.

"Right, gents," announced the Lieutenant as he walked into the room, "as you were, don't stand up ... Lennie! ... have this." He held out his hand with a package. Sanderson moved off the bed and took the package.

"Stevo!" ... Stevens likewise collected a package and finally Wilkins. "There's a grand in cash in each package, plus, a post-dated cheque that makes the balance. You can't present the cheques yet; the money needs to clear. It's very important that you don't flash the cash or people will start asking questions. It's not that there's a lot to spend it on here anyway."

"What about Astley?" piped up Wilkins.

"There's no need for him to be here. He opted out, his choice … cover story now. Why are the three of you here and not marching up and down the square?"

"'Cos you love us, boss," chuckled Lennie Sanderson.

"Alright, don't push it. You are here because I've asked you to do some officer's mess duties, basically waiters for an up-and-coming mess cocktail party. You will be paid for it out of mess funds, and it will stop the others asking awkward questions, so you will have to agree. It won't be that bad. Okay, chaps?"

"Yeah, it makes sense," agreed Lennie Sanderson.

"Alright, off you go and join the others with the platoon on the square."

The three trundled off slowly, no need to rush for a session of square bashing. They were quietly deep in thought, thinking about the wealth they now had acquired.

Belfast 11th July 2002

"How're we doing, Mark? asked DS Pat Connelly,

"Plenty of calls, Sarge, but soon as we get to the Timex watch we hit a brick wall," replied DC Mark Brookes. Pat continued "I am going to order a search of the area as it's been maybe up to thirty years since the body was dumped in the lake, but you never know."

"What about the DI?" questioned DC Brookes.

"We're struggling and anything is worth trying. We'll start where the body was found and work outwards. I want you to get metal detectors, as many as you can locate. There's just a remote chance we might get lucky."

"I'm on to it now, Sarge," replied an enthusiastic DC Brookes.

Pat Connelly took a large breath as he made his way to DI James Walsh's office. He updated the DI with the latest news, which wasn't a lot and told him about the search he was organising. "It seems like we are clutching at straws, Pat."

"We need a break, Guv; we're getting sod all. Yet there is something about this case that's all wrong. I will ask the media to keep pushing for any info regarding a missing person … with a Timex watch, and that's another thing, why the right wrist for the watch?"

"Beats me, Pat, just keep at it and say hello to Sheila for me."

"Thanks, Guv, will do," and with that last remark, DS Connelly left the office, gently closing the door.

Later that day Pat arrived home. Sheila was half expecting him, so it wasn't too long before they were both supping tea. They lived in semi-detached house just outside Bangor. It was their dream home, not far from the coast and a great community. "Good day or okay day?" enquired Sheila.

"Not bad, a little frustrating with the case I'm involved with at the mo."

"What's the problem then?"

"A watch, believe it or not. Why does someone wear their watch on the right-hand, love?"

"That's easy. ... if you are left-handed, that is your dominant hand, then, you are more likely to wear your watch on your right hand. Some cultures have a respect for the importance of the right hand and will wear a watch on that hand. Why? ... I haven't a clue, oh, another one, sometimes the military do but I don't know why?"

"Bloody hell, Sheila, you're full of surprises."

"I'm not just a pretty face, Patrick ... I've got to get on with dinner, so put the telly on for the news, ta."

"Yeah," Pat replied now deep in thought. Being left-handed made sense, how come he never thought of that. It's pretty obvious now, and the culture thing he dismissed as he didn't think his corpse was associated with wagga wagga or voodoo. And why would military personnel wear watches on a different hand? He needed to find the answer to that one, just for curiosity.

The next day before driving to work he decided to phone a mate who was once in the Ulster Defence Regiment. He put the question to his mate, Andy, who had served a good twelve years. "Yes, Pat, some guys used to do that to improve their aim. They reckoned it gave a better control of the gun. I never did as I didn't really think it mattered."

"Thanks for that, Andy. Sorry to phone you this time of the morning."

"No problem, mate, see ya." Andy put the phone down thinking what a strange question to be asking at this time of the morning. However, it did get Pat thinking.

Arriving at his desk later, DS Pat Connelly summoned DC Brookes. "Hi, Mark, I want you to contact the media sources and mention that our body maybe left-handed. It's a shot in the dark but let's see how it pans out."

"Okay, Sarge," replied DC Brookes.

"Also, add maybe ex-military."

"What! How did you work out that, Sarge?"

"Again, it's just a hunch, but I'm throwing everything at this." Pat thought it's all or nothing. It's been a couple of days and nothing. Even the SOCO team haven't triumphed. "Sod it," the DS muttered, as he waded to a WPC sitting at her desk. "Get me the SOCO team, Nancy, I need to have a word," said a frustrated DS Pat Connelly.

The following day, Pat reflected on the frustration of the previous day. The SOCO phone call came to nothing and that about topped it.

He was just about to leave the office when he was called by WPC Nancy O'Connell. "Sarge, there's a man on the phone who wants to speak to the man in charge of the body identity."

"Okay, Nancy, I'll take it at my desk thanks … this is Detective Pat Connelly, how can I help you?"

"Hello, my name is, Eamon Dargan, I served with the Irish Rangers back in the seventies. I remember a fella we had in the platoon ... he was the best shot you'd ever seen, and he was left- handed.

The battalion once had a contest, just for fun. No one could beat him, and when I read in the papers about the body that was found, and he wore his watch on his right hand, I thought, bjesus, I bet that could be Tom McGinn."

"Thanks, Eamon, what happened to him or why could it be him?"

"Well, he disappeared. It would have been in 1969. One minute he was there, the next ... gone."

"Do you know when he joined the platoon, Eamon?"

"It would have been late 1967, I think. I know he lived in Carrickfergus if that helps."

"I really appreciate you coming forward, Eamon, you've been a great help. I'll take your number in case I need to get back to you, if that's alright?"

"No problem at all, I'm glad I could help, ye," and with that, Eamon Dargan rang off.

DC Mark Brooks was in the canteen finishing a steak and kidney pie with a wad of brown sauce and a mug of sweet tea when DS Connelly burst in and sat down next to the DC.

"Just had an interesting call from an Eamon Dargan, ex Irish Rangers. We need to find info on a Tom McGinn, it might, and I say, might be our body. I need you to contact army records. See what we can find about Tom McGinn from Carrickfergus around about 1967."

"Sounds like a break at last, Sarge."

"Take your tea with you, and make a start, I want to feed the DI, he's very hungry," replied an impatient Pat Connelly.

He made his way back to the office, opened the door and was greeted with, "Sarge, can you contact PC Andrews at Dromore regarding the search. I think he's found something," said an excited WPC Nancy O' Connell.

PC John Andrews answered the patrol car radio immediately. "Hi, Sarge, we've found a cartridge, I would say ninety nine percent that it's a 7.62-millimetre cartridge. It was found about four feet from the hedge, and fifty yards from the trees near the pond. It's been bagged and not been handled."

"Well done, PC Andrews, I was beginning to think I was on a wild goose chase. Get it back and I will pass it on to ballistics, and I will make sure the DI gets your report."

"Thank you very much, Sarge. I'm leaving now." PC Andrews called to another two constables. "Okay, back to base and make sure we have all the equipment." They soon packed up and were on their way back to the station in Belfast. "Sounds like we have a break at last, Sarge?" commented WPC O'Connell.

"Yep, Nancy, it's nice to see a bit of movement."

There were two WPCs attached to the office and Nancy O'Connell was the senior of the two.

She joined the RUC in 1968 when she was twenty and eventually married a colleague five years later, right amidst *The Troubles*. As she and her husband were both Catholics serving in the RUC, they became a target in their community.

They were intimidated with name calling, and having unpleasant items pushed through their letter box to begin with, until a petrol bomb was thrown at the front door. After that happened, both were given help and were moved to a new, undisclosed location out of the city.

In April 1998 the *Good Friday Agreement* was announced, which gave hope of peace. It was a huge relief for Nancy, husband, and their two children.

British Sector Berlin 1975

Lt Rory Furness sat back down in the armchair placing his cup of coffee on the table to his right. He glanced out of the window of the officer's mess and checked his car on the car park. He thought about the new registration number he was given now he was stationed in Berlin. He had decided that he would soon learn it off by heart.

"Congratulations, Rory, on your promotion, on your way up now."

"Sorry, Brandon, deep in thought, it's the number plates of the car."

"A ruddy nuisance isn't it ... are you up for going to the French sector tonight with Harry and Ben? There's an excellent restaurant 'Pavillion Du' Lac,' highly recommended."

"Sounds good, Brandon, but I have some things to sort out, definitely another time perhaps."

"Okay, Rory, catch you later." A cheerful Brandon left him in peace. At that, Rory Furness rose out of the armchair and made his way to the phone in the mess hall. He dialled a number from a piece of paper. "Oh, hi, could I speak to Lennie please?"

"Just a min ... LENNIE ... he's coming ... yes, Lennie speaking."

"Hello, Lennie." There was a small pause.

"Boss, is that you?"

"Boss! ... Rory to you now, Lennie, you're now a publican, and that makes you the boss, trade okay?"

"Yeah, good. North Camp is okay, plenty of squaddies. Pop in next time you're in the shot."

"Too busy at the moment, Lennie, heard anything from you know who?" whispered Rory.

"Wilko moved to the Bristol area, Stevo's now an HGV driver, believe it or not, I remember him making an arse of a job trying to park a Land Rover and Astley is still in."

"Yeah, Astley, he worries me," said a concerned Rory.

"He won't squeal, I'm sure," reassured Lennie."

"Okay, gotta go now, Lennie. I'll stay in touch." Rory furtively put the phone back on the hook.

The deal he made with the patrol haunted him. There were sleepless nights, waking up in cold sweats and the dreams. Phoning Lennie could reassure him for a while, but he wished he could go back in time and change the past.

Belfast 12th July 2002

It didn't take long for ballistics to confirm that the cartridge was from a 7.62mm round. Any chance of fingerprints seemed remote, due to time and the outdoor environment.

However, the approach of an optimistic looking DC Brookes looked promising. "Sarge! I've just had a returned call from the army records department. Lance corporal Thomas McGinn number 23995101 from Carrickfergus joined in 1967."

"And ..."

"That's it, Sarge."

"I mean ... when did he get out?"

"Don't know ... they couldn't give me that information."

"Well, that can't be right, they must have lost ... unless ... he ... disappeared. That's what Eamon Dargan said, the ex-Irish Rangers soldier. I need to have another word with him. Come on, you can come with me. I've got his address,"

"Right, Sarge, Can I drive?"

***

"Can I get you fella's a drink?" asked Eamon Dargan as he ushered the two detectives into the living room. "A coffee, two sugars would be fine, thanks," replied DS Connelly.

"A tea please, no sugar," replied DC Brookes.

Later with their hot drinks the DS spoke. "Mr Dargan, or can I call you, Eamon?"

"Eamon's fine, detective."

"Okay, Eamon, I want you to think back to the days when Tom McGinn went missing. Was there anything unusual that happened, or some strangers around who were unknown to you before Tom disappeared?" All three sat in silence.

"I can't think of anything really, the day of the shooting competition was a bit special. Those of us who took part posed for photos, and after that we were treated to a dustbin full of cold beers chilled with ice and I couldn't forget that; the RSM was dishing out the beers and," he started to chuckle, "not all RSM's are as bad as they are portrayed in films."

"Go back a minute, was Tom on the pictures with you?"

"Yes, he was the champion, do you want to see the picture?"

"Please, Eamon."

Five minutes later, Eamon Dargan was rummaging through an old shoe box full of photographs. "Ahhh," triumphed Eamon, as he held the prized picture aloft. He passed it over to the detective. Leaning over he placed a finger under a man holding a trophy. "That's Tom McGinn," he announced, "a great lad."

"Can I borrow it, Eamon, it'll be safe with me?"

"Sure, anything to help the boys in blue, or should I say green."

It was nice to hear a comment like that after years of strife the police in Northern Ireland had been through.

Studying the picture, DS Connelly noticed they were in tracksuits as opposed to uniforms. "It was a Whit bank holiday when the families were invited. After the competition, we had an all-ranks dance held in the NAAFI. Yes ... it was a day to remember."

The two detectives later said their goodbyes, and thanks for the drinks, and hastily made their way back to base.

WPC Jenny Corbett was waiting for the arrival of the two detectives as she had been pre-warned of an important update. "Jenny, we have a picture possibly of the body in the lake. Can you contact our media sources and ask them to publish this picture of the man with the trophy, not the others in the picture; tell them that, the police want to know about the whereabouts of a Tom McGinn. If he's out there alive or officially dead, we can then rule him out regarding the body found in the Dromore pond."

"Will do, Sarge."

"Where's Nancy today?"

"One of her children fell ill at school, and she's gone to collect both children. So, it's just me," she said proudly.

Jenny was young, only twenty-seven and very attractive. She certainly caught the attention of her male colleagues. However, Detective Inspector Walsh wasn't too impressed, so she was given some advice about conducting herself around the office, which went in one ear and out of the other. She just loved the attention.

"This will set the cat amongst the pigeons, Mark," announced DS Connelly who was right, but not in the way he thought.

The next day DS Pat Connelly arrived in his office and was met by an eager WPC Nancy O'Connell. "Morning, Sarge, the SOCO team leader has just phoned, could you return the call?"

"Thanks, Nancy." The DI dialled the number, and the Prof answered.

"Morning, Pat, the dental records confirm that Tom McGinn is your body, and that's not all. I have received a report from ballistics. The cartridge your boys found is a 7.62mm, and I can imagine an AK47 came to mind, however the cartridge is 51mm in length. That's a longer cartridge than a 39mm size used by an AK47."

"What weapon uses that cartridge then, Prof?"

"L1A1 SLR British army." Silence from both men.

"I wasn't expecting that, Prof," replied a very surprised DS Pat Connelly, the Prof continued, "an army weapon can fall into a terrorist group, it does happen.

I know of a true story of a group of squaddies stopping off in a cafe in the middle of a county. When they finished their tea and bacon butties, off they went leaving a rifle in a corner where they were sitting. Ten minutes later a soldier returned in a panic and collected his gun. A soldier told me that."

"I don't know what to think, Prof. I have some thinking to do now. Bye, Prof." DS Connelly sat down at his desk with his right elbow on the desktop and his chin in his palm of his hand. It's time to update Detective Inspector Walsh.

The Black Country 12th July 2002 West Midlands

The Black Country earns its name from several collective towns that mined coal from the many pits. This in turn powered the factories and furnaces that sprung up.
Canals and railways were built to transport the goods all over the globe. The Industrial Revolution was born, and the smoke and soot in this huge area was given this unusual name.
The present day, roads and motorways are now the main form of transport throughout the Black Country, same as any other part of the United Kingdom. So, people need to learn to drive, and that's what Derrick Astley decided to do, become a driving instructor.
He left the army in 1978, as he decided against signing on. He had served nine years in the colours and could leave. For the next three years he would still be in the reserves.
Reserve soldiers can be brought back to serve in a national emergency. Derrick, unlike many ex-force's personnel, settled well into civvy life. He had a job he loved, working for himself and home was a semi-detached in the Wolverhampton area.
The morning of July the 12th was like any other Friday. His wife Mary served out breakfast for him, herself, and their son. Their son was still in his bedroom. "If he doesn't hurry

up, he'll be late for college and he hasn't had his breakfast yet," said Derrick. Mary gave a very loud piecing shout, "Johnathan?"

"Okay, okay," came back the reply. Derrick was gazing over the headlines of the morning paper. Then he saw it. At that moment Johnathan rushed in and grabbed his toast. "Bye, Mom, bye, Dad, see you tonight."

The door closed with a clatter leaving Derrick and Mary alone.

"Can you sit down for a moment, love; I need to talk to you about something."

"What is it, Derrick, you're worrying me?"

"Read this." He passed the newspaper over on the table with his finger pressed on the article.

"What's it got to do with you, Derrick?"

"Something I was sworn to secrecy many years ago, before I met you. The officer in charge of our patrol accidently killed a man but broke all the rules of engagement. To save his career, he bought off the lads with a large amount of money. Except me. I didn't want any part of it, so I refused the money, however I was snookered into not reporting the officer, by swearing in front of the others to keep mum. Not my finest moment, and now after all these years, the body has turned up."

"Isn't there anyone you can speak to?"

"I told you; I'm snookered. They were my mates, and I would be betraying them if I grassed them up, besides ... I could end up propping up the M54 extension."

"That wouldn't happen, Derrick surely, you're being stupid now."

"The officer, he's still in. I've kept tabs on him since leaving. He's alive and kicking as a Lt Colonel. He comes from a very wealthy family, and his father made it to a General ... and he owns a large armaments factory in the South of England. So, I don't want to make enemies with that lot as well as my old platoon. The best thing to do is to keep my head down. I haven't killed anybody anyway."

"You sound like a coward, Derrick. All you need to do is make an anonymous phone call and help the police bring this officer to justice. This shit gets away with it by using his wealthy family's money." Mary's angry words hit Derrick hard.

"A coward is that what I am then?" he said to himself.

He drove off to work with his wife's words going round and around in his head, till he decided on what he must do.

Northern Ireland 1973

The patrol walked off to rendezvous with the ambulance.

Rab had been watching the patrol since their arrival announced by the crack of the SLR rifle. He had to make a quick decision.

He decided to take a fifty-fifty chance and pre-empt their plan of locating the ambulance. He retreated to the lake and found the bush camouflaging a hidden motor bike with a helmet attached to the handlebars. He pushed the bike down the path in silence, not wanting to alert the patrol.

Rab had heard nearly every word that was spoken and saw everything. That the patrol leaders planned to cover up the killing of Rab's associate, took him back, and was totally unexpected, especially as the patrol leader was an officer.

The patrol had ruined the operation, which had taken months of planning, but for now it was important to get to the main road and hopefully pick up and follow the ambulance. With luck, he would find the hospital, the ward, the bed, and the man in it.

Once he had the names, he would get out of the hospital and collect the transit van, load the bike in the back, then return to the woods, locate the M21 sniper rifle and the other helmet, dump the rifle in the water as planned, back to the transit, drive to Larne and then the ferry to Stranraer. What a balls up, all because his associate wanted a dump in private. Not the SAS way.

His associate was there for two reasons only. Probably one of the best shots in the UK and a £100,000 payday.

Now, it was back to his boss. The boss would decide what happens next, at least he would have a list of five names of the patrol, thanks to a very gullible Private Astley.

Put on a white coat and walk around with a clip board, and it's amazing what people will say to you.

Thirty minutes later at the hospital ward. "Ah, Private Astley, had a rough night on patrol then? Never mind, we'll soon sort you out. What was your officer's name?"

"What again? … I just told the doctor with the bushy beard; he's got all the names."

Belfast July 13th 2002

DS Connelly knocked Detective Inspector Walsh's door. "Come in, Pat." The Inspector was accompanied by two men in suits. "I was just about to send for you. These two gentlemen are from the home office in London, and they need to speak to both of us. I emphasise just the both of us, no one else."

"Okay then, sir," replied a mystified DS Connelly.

"I'm James Hawthorn and my colleague, Peter Thompson." They exchanged handshakes during the introductions.

"Sorry, but your investigations are moving into our domain. We need you to put a D notice on the publication of the picture of Tom McGinn. Basically, he is no longer Tom McGinn. We recruited him, shall I say for his talents." explained James Hawthorn, who appeared to be in the controlling seat.

"But he's dead now."

"Yes, and that's how we would like to leave it. You see, Detective Sergeant Connelly; we gave him a new identity, and his family were located to a safe location. That's really all you need to know. It is his family we are protecting; my job is to keep them safe. You understand?"

"What about the person or persons who killed him?" asked DS Connelly.

"Feel free to pursue your investigation, detective, we just wanted to draw a line under the publication of the photograph."

"Why was he there then?" enquired the DS.

"Frankly ... we have no idea."

"Thank you, DS Connelly, you can now carry on with your duties," demanded Detective Inspector Walsh. He gave his Inspector a harsh look as he left the office.

"DC Brookes?"

"Sarge."

"In my office now ... what a load of bollocks!"

"What's that, Sarge?"

"In there ... we can't publish McGinn's picture ... D notice," said the fuming DS, "something is being covered up, but I don't know what. I don't want to implicate you as I can't really talk, but I'm bloody angry. Anyway, we carry on ... we are still looking for a killer before anyone else gets in our way."

"Sarge, I was thinking what you said when the body was discovered, about it being an unplanned killing. Not an execution, an unprepared way of disposing of the body, not wanting it to be found. Now we know it was almost certainly an SLR used by the army."

"An accident, DC Brookes?"

"Could be, Sarge, it fits the MO."

"Keep it to ourselves for now, Mark, because what we are suggesting is extremely serious, and we could find ourselves in deep water if we're not careful. We are just speculating nothing more. I could do with a beer, you up for a quick one, Mark?"

"Lead the way, Sarge."

They both left the station for a drink at a nearby pub frequented by the staff of the local nick.

"Sorry about earlier on, Mark. I had the rug pulled from underneath me. If anyone had recognised the picture of Tom McGinn, we might have had a better timeline of his death. However, I think he was well out of it 'till 1971. Fifteenth of February to be precise."

"How come?"

"Remember the coins in his pocket, those were only released after that date and don't forget the Parka jacket. You would be wearing that on a cold day, certainly not in the summer. I need to press the Prof again. I must know how long the body has been in that pool."

"Another pint?" asked the DC.

"No thanks, Mark, time I made tracks. Sheila is cooking a prawn curry tonight and I don't want to be late. Catch you tomorrow."

"Night, see you ... enjoy the curry," Pat smiled.

Colchester 15th July 2002

Lt Colonel Rory Furness made his way up the stairs to his office as usual. "Morning, sir," said his adjutant, as they passed on the stairs, the adjutant presenting an awkward salute. "Have you got my paper?" asked the Colonel.

"On your desk, sir," replied the adjutant. No reply from the Lt Colonel. The adjutant thought all that training at Sandhurst was wasted, 'I'm just a glorified batman'.

The Colonel sat down at his desk and picked up the paper. Any minute now the orderly will be bringing in a cup of coffee as usual. A smart knock on the door and the orderly entered.

"Morning, sir, your coffee."

"Thank you, Corporal Adams." The Corporal exited as efficiently as he had entered.

The Colonel picked up the paper, and placed it on his desk, then glanced at the main news headlines.

French president Jacques Chirac escaped an assassination attempt during the Bastille Day parade. He immediately thought of 'The Day of the Jackal', a film starring Edward Fox. Same place, same event, but a different president.

He turned the page. *The body found in a lake near Dromore confirmed as a suspicious death.*

He pushed the paper down knocking the cup of coffee over the desk. Sitting still for a few seconds, ignoring the spilt coffee, he pushed backwards on his chair and pulled the paper closer, continuing to read the full article. His world came tumbling down, when a knock on the door suddenly brought him back to reality.

"Finished with your coffee, sir?" asked the orderly. There was a pause as the Colonel sat in thought ... "Sir?"

"Sorry, Corporal yes. Can you bring a cloth and wipe my desk, I've spilt the coffee and when you've finished, I don't want to be disturbed, as I need to make some calls... Don't bother bringing another coffee understand?"

"No problem, sir." The orderly left the room, and a very worried Lt Col Furness picked up the phone.

Glasgow 15th July 2002

McCallister was seated at a table in his local pub reading the paper and now attempting the crossword. A glass of heavy (beer), now half full is placed next to a smouldering cigarette in a glass ashtray.

'Macca' enjoys his own company at this time of day with a quiet pint and a paper.

This cannot be said when he's drinking with the lads. The former Black Watch soldier has a reputation as a hard drinker, and a troublemaker if upset by anyone.

At six foot three inches, shaved head and rugged looks, he's best left alone. He had suited army life, as he excelled at most things, including obeying orders, but after a drink, he could easily lose his temper, and when that happened, it took a brave man to calm him down.

He had spent just over three years in the regiment when a drinking session turned into a punch up, resulting in one man in hospital and another smashed up with a deformed face. It was one fight too many for his CO and Macca was on his way.

However, it wasn't long before Macca was recruited into a shady mercenary group and soon doing what he liked best, fighting. He had a few trusted contacts that were useful when he was free of the contract jobs, and presently he was available, and today was his lucky day as Bob the barman called from the bar. "Macca, call for you."

"Hi Mac, Rab here, I've got something here you might like. Can you call round?"

"Give me an hour, and I'll be there." Macca gulped the rest of his drink. "See ya, Bob," and left the pub.

Rab Anderson, a former SAS trooper who was now nearly sixty. His army career finished in 1968 when he was deemed unfit due to a wound from an AK47 in a fire fight. Rab wasn't a rufty-tufty paratrooper, but a very intelligent soldier who could handle any weapon. Also, very fit and could use his brain to weigh up any situation.

He had no interest in being an officer as he was constantly asked to consider it.

Shortly after arriving in civvy street, he was approached by a mysterious person with an interesting proposition. Rab was escorted to meet a man at a hotel, who offered him clandestine employment, well paid security work, no questions asked. Rab took the job.

He never got to see the mystery man's face as they sat in darkness, except for the light facing Rab. There was no doubt in Rab's mind. This mystery man was military or ex-military, so he called him Boss.

"Hi, Mac, easy job. Want you to follow someone."

"Who is it, Rab?"

"No one important, someone I first met nearly 30 years ago in a Belfast hospital."

"When do I start?"

"Now. I'll give you the full address, it's in the Midlands, near Wolverhampton. His name is Derrick Astley. He has information that we don't want him to spill. Something has occurred and we are worried that he might contact the police. Just keep tabs on him and follow his routine. He works as a driving instructor, and this is his address." He passed Macca an envelope and continued with his orders. "If I feel he isn't a threat, I'll bring you in. Anything you're not happy with, call me, and best take a handgun, just in case. Usual fee, Macca."

Belfast 15th July 2002

"Excuse me, Sarge, I have a caller but won't give me his name, he'll only speak to the person in charge of the body in the lake."
"Sounds interesting, Jenny, I'll take it in my office." WPC Jenny Corbett returned to her desk. "Detective Sergeant Connelly speaking."
"Are you the detective in charge?" asked the caller.
"Yes, can I ask for your name?" replied the DS.
"I am not giving you my name but to gain your attention, I can confirm that the man was killed by an SLR rifle on the 20th of November 1973."
"How do you know that?" asked the DS as he at sat bolt upright.
"Because I was there, and I do not want to speak any more on the phone. Listen carefully and write this down," the DS scrambled for a pen, "Hilton Park services, Southbound M6, 2 p.m. this Wednesday the 17th. I'll be sat at a table with two coffees and a Sun newspaper. Ask me if my name is Roy, and I will give you the list."
"List!" replied the detective.
"List of the names of the patrol." Then the phone went dead.

"Hello, hello... it's no good, the man's replaced the phone. DC Brookes, with me, we need to see DI Walsh now." The DC was busy typing. He ceased immediately and followed the DS to the office.

Within a few minutes, all three detectives were discussing the phone call. "I think it's genuine, sir, there was an air of urgency in his voice and fear. He wanted to end the call quickly. Also, he brought up the word patrol, and nobody has mentioned that at all in the investigation," stated the DS.

"A list of the names of the patrol, who are complicit in the death of a man?" said the Detective Inspector who was now puffing away on his pipe.

"Okay, I want both of you on this. Arrange a ferry for tomorrow. DC Brookes, I want you to observe the meeting from a distance because I don't want this chap spooked, so put work clothes on or something to blend in. Order a meal and don't let a cleaner take the dirty plates away."

"Yes, sir."

"I want to get to the bottom of this whole thing, bodies, guns, spooks ... and I've got the chief superintendent in my ear to top it all. Good luck, Pat."

"We will do our best, sir, and keep you updated."

The two detectives departed. Time now to get prepared for Wednesday's trip to the West Midlands.

The West Midlands 17th July 2002

The ferry docked in Stranraer, Scotland. After their car exited the ferry, they began the long road journey to junction 13 on the M6. There after a few stops on the way, DS Connelly decided to take the A499 into Wolverhampton and book into a hotel.

The next day, they were going earlier to the service station to get an idea of the layout. It was decided that this man masquerading as Roy, more than likely lived locally, hence why they were meeting at a service station.

They took a different road out of the town, the A460 to Cannock, joining the M6 at Junction 11 for the very short ride to the exit, at Hilton Park services.

They had a good hour to kill, so they both agreed to separate and keep apart. DC Brookes put the work clothes on. DS Connelly looked at him, and nodded, "Not bad," he said, "let's go, and good luck," he added.

Forty minutes later a man driving a Morris Ital approached junction 11. At the island he turned on to the M6 Southbound, and after the shortest of rides, he then exited the motorway into the Hilton Park services.

He slowly made his way to the eating area and ordered two cups of coffee. Carrying the two coffees, he made his way over to a seat near the window. The restaurant wasn't busy.

He looked at his watch and furtively looked around slowly, to see if there was any sign of the detective.

A couple arrived at the counter, chatting to one another. She was wearing a blue dress, and he was in motorbike leathers.

A lady sitting with two small girls, were about three tables away and a youngish man, maybe in his thirties, was finishing a meal in a corner at the end of the restaurant.

At exactly 2:00 p.m. DS Connelly walked in alone. He stood still and stared at the man on his own, then slowly walked over. "Is your name, Roy?" asked DS Connelly.

"Sit down, detective." The man passed him a coffee.

"No sugar in it, I'm afraid." There was a pause, then, he continued to speak.

"I have lived with this for nearly thirty years. I wanted no part of it. I turned down the money, £10,000 and was threatened not to talk. My life is in danger, detective, and I want you have this list, it's important."

He started to give the detective the envelope containing the names and the army unit, when a voice said, "I'll have that," and a large hand grabbed the envelope from DS Connelly's fingers.

DC Brookes by now was rushing over to the man in bike leathers. He pounced on him and ripped the envelope away. The man in leathers pushed him backwards over a chair, leaving the DC sprawled on the floor.

The woman started screaming, and the girls were crying. Then the sound of a gunshot rang out. The man in leathers had drawn the weapon, pointed it at Astley then pulled the trigger. Astley keeled over after being shot in the middle of his chest. Cordite rose in the air, as the man in leathers knocked chairs and drinks over as he rushed away.

The woman was beside herself, as were the girls behind the counter. DS Connelly by now had moved Astley onto the floor. He located the gunshot wound and shouted to the girls at the counter, to bring him a plastic bag and call an ambulance quickly. He placed the bag over the hole in Astley's chest and kept it there.

"Follow him!" shouted DS Connelly. DC Brookes gave chase, but the man in leathers had a start on him. Outside, he heard a motorbike being started. He ran towards the sound just to see the bike disappear into a service road at the rear of the service station.

He returned to the restaurant. "Sorry, Sarge, he had a bike and rode off at the back down a service road."

"I shouldn't have asked you to chase him 'cos he was armed and dangerous. Can you ask everyone to remain for statements, and get the place closed off?" ordered DS Connelly.

"How is he?"

"I don't know, he's breathing, just about."

After ten minutes, there was the sound of an ambulance arriving. That was followed by a male voice giving instructions in the restaurant. The crew rushed in and took over from the Detective Sergeant. More sirens were heard; this would be the local police. "This is where the shit hits the fan," he muttered to his DC. Then he realised, he still had the list. The gunman only had a bit of the envelope.

The paramedics soon had a drip fitted. "Who patched him up?" asked a paramedic.

"I did what I could. It looked like a sucking wound to the chest."

"You were right. Could you clear a way for us, we are about to leave thanks."

"No problem, you heard him, let's make some space," ordered the DS.

A Chief Inspector from the West Midlands Police had arrived during the chaos, because of the shooting. The SOCO team were already in action. A West Midlands detective was taking statements from the witnesses.

Uniformed police were everywhere, including the parking area. "Why weren't we told anything about this operation?" asked the Chief Inspector.

"To be honest, sir, it wasn't an operation. We are investigating a killing over the water, and this fella contacted us to give information only in person. We had no idea all this would kick off. My DI back in Belfast, DC Brookes there, and myself, are the only ones that knew the location of the meeting."

"Well, it's a joint operation from now. We want this shooter who ever he is. We know he has a Scottish accent according to the female witness over there and we have a good description. George! ... over here. This is my Detective Inspector I'd like you to work with."

The DI walked over towards them. "DI George Lane, gents."

George Lane was an impressive figure. Six feet and 3inches tall. He was of Jamaican heritage. His parents had settled in Wolverhampton back in the 1950s.

There were the usual introductions then DI George Lane continued where the Chief Inspector left off.

"Glasgow, that's the accent the female witness states. She reckons that the chatting up he did when they were at the counter was a ploy."

"A ploy?" queried DS Connelly.

"Yes, to blend in, as if they knew each other."

"Clever bastard," piped in DC Brookes.

"I've got uniform knocking doors, near the exit of the service road, which is mainly farmhouses and lanes. SOCO have the cartridge, so we should have the round, when it's removed from the victim. There's a security camera in the car park area, so we'll see if we can get access. Details of the crime, will be broadcasted on this evening's news: on both main channels."

"They don't hang around over here do they, Sarge," remarked DC Brookes.

"Yes, but how did the shooter know? Who tipped him off or employed him?"

An hour later, the crime scene was still a hive of activity, as a voice shouted to DI Lane. "Sir, we've just had a call from uniform. A girl riding a horse in a paddock saw a man loading a motorbike into a green van, it might be a transit. He drove off towards the M6 junction."

"Junction 11 ... If he has come down from Glasgow, that's a long hard drive on a bike, but in a van ... alert all forces to be on the lookout for a green van, no markings, possible transit, registration unknown. Male driver with shaved head, likely Glaswegian, has a firearm and dangerous. Possibly northbound on the M6," instructed DI Lane.

"That would put him in the Manchester area by now, but he doesn't realise that we know he's driving a van, and that may be his undoing," said DS Connelly.

The Chief Inspector returned after the press briefing. "I'm returning now to the station. Keep me updated please, George."

"Yes, sir," replied DI Lane.

M6 Preston 17th July 2002

A patrol car travelling northbound on the M6 pulled onto the outside lane, avoiding some commuter traffic that had built up. The two officers were discussing football, when the officer in the passenger seat cried out. "Green van inside lane, pull back a bit." The driver eased into the middle lane. "Let the traffic in the inside catch up, so I can get a butchers at the driver."

"Okay, Len, be careful."

A few vehicles passed inside which brought the driver of the van level. Len studied the driver who was looking straight ahead. "It's him, without a doubt. Drop back and wave the cars behind to pass.

Try and get behind the van with cars sandwiched between and I'll radio control now so they can organise a roadblock."

"I hope you're right, Len, because we won't hear the last of it if we're wrong."

The radio came to life again. "A roadblock is being put together in Lancaster junction 34. Soon as you pass junction 33, radio in. Armed officers will be situated at various spots at the roadblock at junction 34. Before you get to the roadblock, we will attempt to block the van in a box. After junction 33, patrol cars will join the motorway. One will get behind the van, another in front, one by the side, and one in the breakdown lane. We will wave him down, to pull him to a stop. Armed officers will be on all patrol cars. Hopefully, they will not be required.

The motorway will be closed behind you as soon as you pass junction 33. All you need to do is keep sight of the van, let us do the rest."

"Will do," replied Len."

Macca, the van driver, noticed the lack of traffic since passing junction 33. He screwed his eyes up, as he peered into the rear view and wing mirrors.

Then he saw the mass of flashing lights coming into view. "Oh fuck!" The game was up, or was it? There were cars around him, which were continuing their journey as normal.

Macca anticipated what they were about to do and put his foot down full on the accelerator. He turned the van left onto the hard shoulder of the motorway, and now he was undertaking the traffic to his right.

The patrol cars with lights fully on, and their sirens blasting, had now caught up with the traffic. Macca was having none of it, and now the speedometer was reading 90 mph. His intention was to use the traffic to his right, to keep the patrol cars off him, however, he didn't consider what a breakdown lane is used for.

He was busy watching the mirrors, the traffic, the little girl in the rear car window waving, then nothing ... Macca was gone.

"Jesus!" Len shouted as their car jolted upwards, just as they passed the explosion of the green van. The van had ploughed into the back of an articulated lorry.

Smoke, fire and van parts were strewn all over the road.

The car with the little girl inside swerved off to left of the articulated lorry, its windscreen smashed with debris. All traffic pulled to a standstill except the outside lane.

Patrol cars pulled up still with sirens and lights blazing.

The driver of the lorry was coming from the grass verge, open mouthed at what he had just witnessed in front of him.

A coach veered over from the middle lane and pulled to a halt in the shoulder lane, in front of the car with the smashed windscreen, that had come to a halt.

The southbound lane had traffic crawling along, as drivers were gazing at the carnage, and smoke, left over from the crash.

A mother was left consoling her little girl, who was sobbing her heart out. Blood from the mother's face, cut with windscreen glass, was smeared on to her daughter as she hugged her.

The police were scattered around sorting out the chaos. Officers on radios; directing traffic; helping motorists; clearing debris and checking the van of McCallister ... what was left of it!

Five minutes later, an ambulance with its two-tone siren still blaring, pulled up, and the paramedics exited quickly making their way to the hard shoulder, where the car with the smashed windscreen had stopped. They immediately began treating the occupants of the car.

Len and his driver were commended later for their vigilance and professional actions.

The West Midlands 18th July 2002

Detective Sergeant Connelly, and Detective Constable Brookes, had just finished breakfast at their hotel when DI George Lane joined them.
"Morning, chaps, I thought you would like a full update before you leave the Black Country. Our shooter was a nasty piece of work from Glasgow, she was right," referring to the female witness.
"Known as Macca, real name, James McCallister. A man who was for hire. Anything unpleasant it seems, and as for the driver of the articulated lorry ... would you believe, pulled over because he had the shits."
"I bet he ran back when he saw what happened to his wagon," laughed DC Brookes. They all broke into laughter.
"Okay, we shouldn't be laughing should we, after all, a man has been shot who ... I'm pleased to say, is now out of danger.
We now know who he is, Derrick Astley, a local guy who's a driving instructor, and now under police guard, at New Cross Hospital. His wife and son are by his bedside now. Mary, his wife is very distraught and keeps blaming herself for some reason. You may have saved his life by your quick action, Pat."

"If I helped him, I'm glad about that." DS Connelly replied.

"Who would go to so much trouble to send that piece of work to stop him talking?" asked the DI.

"This!"

DS Connelly held up the list. "This list contains the names of an army patrol that allegedly killed a man then covered up the killing. Derrick Astley was a member of this patrol but didn't want to take part in a cover up. He turned down the offer of a bribe of £10,000."

"£10,000, wow, who offered that sort of money?" asked the DI.

"The patrol commander, 2nd Lieutenant Rory Furness."

"Did he send the hit man?" again the DI asked.

"That we don't know, but what we need to do, is find the other three men of the patrol. Their lives I believe, are now in danger, and they are also potential witnesses."

"Well, it's a joint operation now, so our end will make a start today. Just one thing, Pat?"

"What's that?"

"The list ... please."

Belfast 19th July 2002

Both forces now had the names of the unit and the patrol:

*2nd Lt Rory Furnace,
L/Cpl Lennie Saunders,
Privates Russell Wilkins,
Jack Stevens, and Derrick Astley.*

The list is the rank they had held, back on the 20th of November 1973, which was pointed out by DS Connelly back at his office. "This information is once again from army records, DC Brookes. It won't give us all the answers but it's a start and make sure we have their original home addresses. We need to know where they came from, it might help."
"Yes, Sarge."

Glasgow 19th July 2002

"What the fucking hell just happened?" asked the angry voice at the other end of the phone.
"Macca blew it he must have panicked. Everything was planned, a bike for a quick getaway, and a change of vehicle, so he must have been seen. All we will know now, is what the press will publish. The police are not going to tell them everything are they?" said Rab, who tried to reassure the boss that all was not lost.
"Find the patrol before the police do and try and make it look like an accident ... at least we don't have to worry about the Lance Corporal, Lennie Sanderson. So that's one less."
"Alright boss, one less helps. I'm on it." Rab replaced the phone.
Time to get to work starting with the man in the hospital.

***

At a pub a few miles away two detectives walked in.
"Are you the landlord?" asked one.
"Yes, how can I help you?" Showing their warrant cards, the same detective spoke.
"Macca drinks here, doesn't he?"

"On occasions, he sometimes pops in."

"Come off it, this is his bloody office, now, what time is he in?"

"Okay, about 9:30 tonight, you might catch him."

"You don't know do you?" said the second detective.

"Know what?"

"Macca was killed on the M6."

"That's a bit of a sick joke, isn't it?"

"Read the papers tomorrow, it's no joke." There was a short pause then the detective continued. "I want a word with Rab, his mate to tell him the bad news."

"I don't know anyone by that name," said the flustered landlord.

"Sure, you do, your wee lassie barmaid heard the name when he was on the phone. Now, no more pissing around, so talk or no more lock-ins."

"All I know is that this Rab offers, I mean did offer Macca work. I've never seen him, but I heard that this guy was ex special forces. Macca talked a lot when he was really pissed. The SAS remark slipped out."

"Thank you for your co-operation, sir, have a good night." The two detectives left.

They went back the station and passed the new information to West Midlands and Northern Ireland police

Northern Ireland 20th July 2002

Armed with this latest information, that a former SAS soldier was giving instructions to a beast like Macca, was worrying for DS Connelly and his DI. "The man who was shot recently at Hilton Park sadly died last night."

"What!" a shocked DI Walsh retorted.

"No, he didn't, but that's what we need to put out. Our new suspect, Rab, will take over now and he's no fool. Derrick Astley is no longer safe in the hospital. If he's well enough to be moved, then that's what we must do."

"There's an armed guard on duty at all times, Pat."

"That's no match for an ex-SAS man. He will be in and out within seconds, Guv."

"Okay, that might be a bit drastic, tricking the press, so how about moving him to an unknown location, so he can recover, but ... still carry on with the impression that we are still guarding our wounded man in the ward."

"Alright, Pat, I'll speak to West Mids, and tell them of your plan. It could be the second time you have saved the man's life."

West Midlands 20th July 2002

Detective Inspector George Lane arrived at New Cross Hospital. He glanced at his at his watch and continued to the private ward where Derrick Astley was recovering.

By his bedside sat his wife Mary, who was holding her husband's hand. "Hello, Mrs Astley, my name is Detective Inspector George Lane. Could I have a private word with you?"

"Of course, detective, what is it?"

"Call me George, Mrs Astley, please. Can we just move over to the small room across the corridor?" She followed the Inspector to the small room. He closed the door, and they both sat down. "Firstly, let me tell you how brave your husband is. The information he has given the police is invaluable. Hopefully, it will give us enough to solve a conspiracy and maybe more, so please convey our thanks to Derrick later. Now, there is something else," he then noticed the tears, "are you alright, Mrs Astley?"

"Sorry, George, I'm blubbing again, I said he was a coward and look what's happened."

"Now, don't blame yourself, we all say things that sometimes we regret."

"Please continue ... I'll be fine."

"As I was about to say, we want to move your husband to an unknown location, only as a precaution, just to be on the safe side. I want to keep the appearance up that he's still in the recovery room with an armed guard. We are going the extra mile to protect Derrick, only till this investigation is concluded."

"Why, I don't understand? You have the information now. Why would they still come for him?"

"*They*, is a good word because we don't know who they are, trust us, Mrs Astley, let us get to the bottom of this. Now, I must go and thank you for your patience and understanding. We will let you know where he will be, but you must keep up the pretence that he is here in New Cross. Goodbye now."

"Thank you, George." They both went their separate ways. The Inspector will now put the plan into action.

Belfast 20th July 2002

"The army records don't really tell us much, but we now know that our lieutenant is a now a Lt Colonel. He's come a long way hasn't he, Sarge?"

"Looks like it, Mark, what about the others?"

"Well, we know about Astley, that checks out. Private Russell Wilkins left the army soon after, January 18th, 1974; Followed by Lance Corporal Sanderson January 30th, 1974; and lastly Private Jack Stevens the 15th of March 1974.

Wilkins from Bristol, Sanderson from Farnborough, Stevens from Burnley."

"Good, Mark. They all left nearly at the same time, and I wonder if a large amount of money had something to do with it. However, we can't assume that they all returned to their original homes. Now we'll try the electoral roll of each area and see what comes up."

"On it now, Sarge," said the DC.

"DS Connelly?" WPC Jenny Corbett called out.

"Yes, Jenny?"

"Phone for you, DI George Lane, West Midlands."

"Got it, Jenny ... hello Inspector, Pat Connelly speaking."

"Hi Pat, some info for you, good news is, Derrick Astley has been talking. He kept in touch with Russell Wilkins, and he last spoke to him about eighteen months ago. He lives in Kewstoke, Western-Super-Mare. Married, with two teenage kids. Astley can't remember the name of the road. Fortunately, it's no problem as the Somerset police force, are going to his home now as I'm talking to you. They are going to put the family in protective custody, also there's one more thing. Derrick Astley remembered something that might be useful. On the night of the shooting, Sanderson mentioned buying a pub now he had the money, but it might be all talk though."

DS Connelly then updated DI Lane with the news regarding Rory Furness and thanked him and replaced the phone.

"Just Lennie Sanderson and Jack Stevens the last to locate now," remarked the DS.

"Why aren't we picking up Furness, Sarge?" asked DC Brookes.

"First thing, Mark, he's a suspect, and could be the one that's employing this man, Rab. But we have no proof yet. Also, will the patrol want to testify against him? They might not now, after what's happened to Astley. So ... we don't want to lose any men of the patrol. They are crucial."

The detective paused a little. "There's still something bothering me with the whole thing Mark."

"What's that?"

"Why! ... why go to so much trouble and how come they have been one step in front of us. How did they know about the Hilton Park rendezvous with Astley? Something else is going on here and I haven't got a bloody clue."

West Midlands 21st July 2002

"Thanks for getting back so quickly, appreciate it, bye. Okay everyone, I have just been speaking to Hampshire police, and they have been putting the word about Lennie Sanderson and a pub," said DI George Lane, "and we have a result. Lennie Sanderson died in a car crash in 1998. He ran a pub in North Camp, Farnborough, so we can now cross Lennie Sanderson off the list. That's one less to worry about so back to it everyone."

Unbeknown to DI Lane, Rab Anderson had arrived at New Cross Hospital following a long drive from Glasgow.

He parked his car in the car park and went to the boot retrieving a small holdall. A & E seemed the best place to start. Playing the role of a police detective, Rab was very convincing.

He flashed a forged police identity card to a junior doctor. "Sorry to bother you, but I'm looking for my Detective Inspector. He's here with a patient with a gunshot wound so can you direct me in the right direction please?"

"Try the critical care unit ward B9," replied the helpful junior doctor.

"Thank you for your help." Rab marched off to find B9 in the maze of corridors of New Cross hospital.

After about 15 minutes, he turned a corner in a corridor and spotted an armed police officer complete with flak jacket. He back tracked and walked down another passage till he spotted a sign for toilets.

He entered, and after five minutes, a doctor exited, complete with stethoscope around the neck, white coat and a well-worn clip board, but no holdall as Rab had left that in the toilet. The glasses worn by Rab, masquerading as a doctor, were dark rimmed and on the coat a name tag was attached, completing the disguise.

Returning to the room where the armed policeman stood, Rab approached, pushing a stretcher trolley. "Sorry, Constable, but I need to pop the trolley in here. Won't be a tick."

Rab wasn't going to wait for a reply; he didn't allow the officer time to think. By the time the police officer protested, Rab was in, parked the trolley and out again. "Sorry to disturb you, all done." The officer peered into the room and saw the parked trolley. He felt relieved, as everything looked normal.

Rab had seen what he needed to see. A poor attempt at trying to trick him, believing a patient was in there being treated for a gunshot wound. A mannequin covered in sheets, no monitors or drip line and where was the clip board at the bottom of the bed? Rab had assessed it in two seconds. As he suspected, they had moved Derrick Astley. "Time for plan B; find the wife and follow … boring," he muttered under his breath.

The police sergeant arrived later to relieve the constable. "Where's that trolley come from, Constable?"

"A doctor bought it in, Sarge."

"No one is allowed in under no circumstances."

"He came straight out, Sarge."

"That's because he saw what he needed to see, you plonker. All the staff have been warned to stay away from this room and stay there while I inform the DI." Back at the station DI Lane was on the phone. "Thank you, Sergeant." He replaced the receiver. "Looks like we have another hit man on our patch. He was sniffing around at the hospital earlier. I'm off out now and take the guard off the room as it's pointless now."

George Lane left the station as he felt he needed to speak to Mary Astley in person.

***

"Thank you for inviting me, Mrs Astley, can we sit down somewhere?"

"Certainly Inspector, sorry, George, let's go to the living room. Cup of tea or coffee?"

"Tea please, two sugars, thanks."

Later when they were settled drinking tea, the inspector spoke. "I will come straight to the point. We now know that an associate of the man who shot your husband was reconnoitring the hospital today looking for Derrick."

"Oh my god, why? … hasn't he suffered enough?"

"I know this is very distressing for you, but I would like you to do something for me."

"What is it you want me to do?"

"Help me take this man off the streets, so your lives can get back to normality.

This man is clever, and now he knows Derrick has been relocated, I think he realises the only chance to find him is you. He'll need to follow you as he suspects that eventually you'll want to visit your husband, which of course is true. I would like you to go to a hospital, but not the one where Derrick is. All you do is walk into the hospital entrance and follow a lady in a yellow coat, and if he doesn't show, we do it the next day, and again. Visiting time could be afternoon, or evening, we can work around your employment. Will you do it, Mrs Astley?"

"Will I be safe, George?"

"I think so, you will be visible all the time, besides, he needs you to locate Derrick. Act like you would normally do ... park up at the hospital and don't look around, just walk straight ahead and above all, trust the police to take this man off the streets. We have a special team waiting in the wings for the nod."

"All right, I'll do it," sighed Mary Astley.

"Thank you, Mrs Astley, and it's very brave of you. We start tomorrow, so I would like you now to see the route to the hospital, it's not too far away. You will drive the same route everyday you go."

DI Lane sat down and produced a map of the route and then left to put the plan into operation.

Later back at the station, the Chief Inspector listened intently to the briefing presented by DI Lane. "George why are you not using one of our WPCs to masquerade as Derrick Astley's wife?" asked the Chief.

"The man we're dealing with is a very different character than our Glasgow thug, sir. He's cool and calculating, and the bad news is, according to a report from two Glasgow detectives, he may be an ex-SAS man, who would smell a rat straight away. If he is as good as I think he is, this man will be watching the movements of Mrs Astley wherever she goes. From her journey to work; back home; the shops; the hairdresser and so on if you get my drift. He won't move till he's one hundred percent sure so we must be on the ball. Slowly, slowly catch a monkey. We have placed an experienced team on the operation, now we must be patient."

"Well best of luck then, George."

"Thank you, sir."

Burnley 22nd July 2002

Jack Stevens was the last man of the patrol to be unaware of the news. A body was found in a lake at Dromore, Northern Ireland, and he knew nothing about it. For the last two weeks, he had been abroad with his wife, Jo, on a holiday in Skiathos, a Greek island in the Aegean Sea.

They had arrived back at Manchester airport in the previous two hours, and the couple were now finally back home in Burnley. Back to normality and the first job, unpack, and make two mugs of tea.

Second job, check the fishpond and remove any dead fish if there are any. The pond is at its deepest point five foot deep as Koi prefer that depth, particularly in the colder weather.

Jo was in the lounge busy opening the two holdalls, searching for dirty washing. "Where is he, I'm trying to unpack and sort things out and he's more concerned about his precious fish," Jo protested.

"Jack!" she bellowed at full volume, "Where the hell are you?... I need some help here with the unpacking," ... no reply, "for fuck's sake give me a hand, sod the fish."

She marched out to the back garden then let out an enormous scream, as she was confronted with Jack lying face down in the fishpond.

Belfast 22nd July 2002

"Sarge, we now have the address of Jack Stevens, in an area of Brierfield, Burnley."

"Well done, Mark, ring the nick at Burnley and give them all the info, I'll be in my office."

"Okay, Sarge," replied DC Brookes already picking the phone up.

"Nancy! any chance of a cuppa?" cried out the DS.

"Here we go again," whispered Nancy.

Sat in his office the cup of tea was very welcome, until DC Brookes burst through the door. "Sarge, he's dead! Jack Stevens was found dead at home, lying face down in the fishpond.

They had just returned from a holiday abroad, opened the house up, his wife started unpacking while he went to see how the fish were. She wondered where he was, so she went to the rear garden and found him dead in the pond."

"Shit, if we had only moved quicker. Let's assume its foul play. Then the killer would have been waiting at the back of the house also, he would have knowledge of the return flight and flight number. Ahead of us again. This changes things now, Mark, so not counting Furness, we have two credible witnesses, and we are lucky with that." He looked at his DC straight into his eyes and spoke slowly, "I think it's now the time, to finally interview Lt Col Rory Furness".

Nancy, the phone number for Lt Col Furness is pinned on the incident board. Can you ring it for me please? and when you're through to him, hand me the phone. Somehow, I don't think he will be pleased to speak to me."

Lt Col Rory Furness was speaking to the RSM about the up-and-coming parade the following month. A knock on the door distracted them. "Come in," barked the Colonel. The orderly entered "Sorry, sir, but there's a call for you from a Detective Sergeant Connelly in Belfast. He's most insistent on talking to you, sir."

The Colonel remained quiet for a moment to collect his thoughts, "alright, RSM, we can pick this up later." The RSM clicked his heels together, gave a smart salute and left the room. "Orderly, put him through."

"Very good, sir," and the orderly left the room.

"How can I help you, Detective Sergeant?"

"Sorry to disturb you, sir but it's most important that I see you."

"Well, what's it about then, I am extremely busy organising a parade at the moment?"

"If I said your life could be in danger, or even a family member, sir, would that make a difference? I could catch a flight to Heathrow tonight and be there perhaps late morning."

"I am intrigued, detective, all right, I shall see you tomorrow. I will make arrangements with the guardroom to let you into the barracks. They will ask to see your warrant card and an escort will accompany you to my office."

"Thank you, sir, and I look forward to meeting you tomorrow." DS Connelly put the phone down, turned around to see that DI Walsh had entered the room. "Flying to Heathrow, Pat? We have a budget you know."

"Sorry, sir, but I need to speak to this colonel. He has no idea that we have the names of the patrol, and the accusation of a cover up of a killing. We only have, at this moment in time, one witness who will testify, and we are lucky that he is still alive. If we can get Russell Wilkins to testify, its game on. The problem we have with Wilkins is; will he admit to taking the money? He might find himself in trouble if he does. But now things are moving fast, so we will interview him later with your permission, sir. There is something else I would like to ask for."

"I have a feeling that I'm not going to like this."

"Going back to the lake, sir, the area that we searched is incomplete in my opinion."

"Where yer coming from, Pat?"

"We didn't look in the water, and yes, the frog men went in but only to bring the body up. We never asked them to look around the area under the water."

"Alright Pat, I give up. I will get the scuba guys to do a search, but I'm sceptical that anything will turn up."

"Thanks, sir, I'll go now and sort myself out for the flight, but before I go, I just need to make a telephone call."

DS Connelly left DI Walsh's office as the DI picked up his pipe and tobacco and continued the routine of smoking his pipe.

The DS dialled a number. "Hi, is that Mrs Sanderson?"

"Speaking."

"My name is Detective Sergeant Pat Connelly speaking from Belfast. Can you spare a moment?"

"How do I know you are a real copper?"

"Ask the operator for the number for PSNI. When you get through ask for DS Connelly in Belfast. That way you will know that I'm the real deal. I'll put the phone down now." After about five minutes the phone rang. "Mrs Sanderson, this is Pat Connelly. I'll now ask you something to do with a case I am working on ... Lennie's car accident, could you tell me a bit about it?"

"Well, that's not quite right."

"What do you mean, Mrs Sanderson?" DS Connelly was puzzled by her answer.

"It was a hit and run. Lennie wasn't driving. The coroner said it was an unlawful killing, because the driver didn't stop, and may have been deliberate."

"Was the driver caught?"

"No, it was at night in a lane. There were no witnesses at all."

"Can you tell me the date?"

"Certainly, Tuesday 6th of October 1998."

"You seem very sure that it was a Tuesday."

"That's because Lennie had a day off and Tuesday was always the worst day of the week with the takings at our pub. Normally Lennie went to the Bell, but that night he went to the Pear Tree."

"What was the reason he changed pubs that night?"

"He was pretty excited, as he was meeting one of his old pals from the regiment. It was nice to see him happy. The pub had been struggling for about 18 months, and it was getting Lennie down. This mate really bucked him up."

"Did he mention any names?"

"No, but he said his mate had got something for him. I asked him what and he said, 'ask no questions and I'll tell no lies.' Said it with a smirk he did."

"Did you tell the police about this friend?"

"I'm not sure, I was all over the place. It's taken a couple of years to get over it."

"I must go now, Mrs Sanderson, but I want to thank you for talking to me. It will help me a lot and I hope that I can, in the future, give you a call and explain everything. Goodbye."

"Bye, detective."

The DI was thinking deeply about the conversation with Mrs Sanderson.

"DC Brookes,"

"Sarge,"

"Before I go, I need you to do something. I would have done it myself, but I don't want to miss the plane. Let's sit down in my office a minute, because you might want to take some notes."

"Okay, Sarge, sounds important."

"It is, Mark, and I will need the information that hopefully you obtain, for my meeting tomorrow, with the colonel. Here we go.

Tuesday 6th of October 1998. The Pear Tree pub near Frimley. In a lane not far from the pub, Lennie Sanderson was killed by a car not long after leaving that pub. It was a hit and run."

"Just a moment, Sarge, I thought he was killed in a traffic accident?"

"We all did, Mark, but now we're looking at past events far more closely. Get hold of the police who dealt with it, they must have interviewed the bar staff at the pub and ask for a copy of any statements taken to be faxed or emailed to you. It doesn't matter how trivial it seems.

Lennie's wife told me that the coroner's report was an unlawful killing, not an accident. Now, I've got to go, and I'll ring when I arrive at Heathrow. I might have to catch you at home. Sorry about that."

"That's alright, Sarge, have a good trip." He decided to leave the thinking till he was seated on the plane. For now, he had some packing to get on with, and his wife Sheila was getting a bit tetchy with these last-minute disappearances.

Burnley 22nd 2002

Driving away from Burnley on the M65 Rab Anderson was feeling pleased with himself.

"That went far better than expected. The flight was on time, and the couple came straight home.

Getting into the rear garden was piece of cake, up and over a six-foot fence, no problem. Wouldn't have done it in daylight though. Hanging around the garden, boring as normal.

No need of a firearm, a cosh was all that was required and an easy exit due to no locks, just two bolts to slide across and Bob's your uncle.

I'll soon be on the M6 back down to the West Midlands or do I go to Bristol."

Heathrow airport evening of 22nd July 2002

"Hi, Mark, I'm still at the airport just about to get a taxi to the hotel. How'd you get on?"
"Well, Sarge it took a bit of time, but I eventually received an email. The pathologist's report was consistent that Lennie sustained injuries hit by a vehicle. Broken femur; broken ribs; punctured lung; and traumatic brain injury. He was dead before the ambulance arrived. A passing car stopped, and the driver found the body lying near edge of the road, and the body was identified by a credit card in his pocket.
A police statement given by a barmaid named as June Smallman." He read out the statement from the email:

The pub was fairly quiet; it usually is on a Tuesday evening. I remembered this man coming into the lounge about 8:30 p.m. He was wearing a leather jacket and jeans. He ordered a pint of beer. He was friendly, but I had never seen him before. He sat down and was reading some papers, not newspapers. There were a few other people sat at tables, so I carried on serving and collecting empties. He later reordered another pint and returned to his table.

Next time I looked his way, a gentleman had joined him. They were talking. The man was dressed in a smart suit. I was waiting for him to order a drink from the bar so I thought I'll collect the empties from another table and ask him what he would like to drink. As I was walking towards them, I saw the gent passing a large envelope to the other man. He placed it on the table, and I couldn't help but notice what was written on it: On her majesty's service. It was a bit bulky, but I have no idea what was in it. I asked the man what he would like to drink, and he replied that he wouldn't be staying. I didn't think he was very friendly.

The man picked up the envelope and put it in his jacket pocket. I remember it well because it was so unusual. It was like something from James Bond. The first man had another drink later and complimented on how good the beer was and said a friendly goodbye.

"Thank you, Mark. The statement of the barmaid is very interesting and that gives me a bit of ammunition for tomorrow. Have a good night, bye."

Detective Sergeant Pat Connelly now made his way to the hotel. He wanted an early night as he needed to have his wits about him tomorrow. He would be facing perhaps his most difficult adversary, ever.

Colchester 23rd July 2002

DS Connelly had finally arrived in Colchester after an hour's trip from London's Liverpool Street Station. He hailed a taxi and made his way to the barracks.
As expected, he was asked to prove his identity and then escorted to meet Lt Colonel Rory Furnace.
Walking through the barracks they passed the square. The RSM (Regimental Sergeant Major) was putting the companies through their paces barking orders. Each company had their own Sergeant Majors also barking orders. DS Connelly could only admire the precision of the marching. Certainly, the best, he thought. "We're here now, sir," announced the escort "the Colonel's office is there."
"Thank you, Corporal." replied the DS, he did recognise military ranks.
At last, for the first time, DS Pat Connelly is now poised to meet the Colonel for the first time. He took a deep breath as he knocked the door. "Come in please," invited the colonel. He stood up as the detective walked in. The colonel spoke first. "Colonel Furness, Detective Sergeant," He held out his hand, and the DS responded by shaking his hand. "Please take a seat, pleasant journey?"
"Very good, thank you, sir. I was just admiring the troops marching on the square, very impressive."

"Thank you, Detective Sergeant. I like to think of them as the finest regiment in the British Army but I'm sure the brigade of guards would disagree. Now, what's this about my life may be in danger?"

"Back in 1973 you were on a tour of Northern Ireland and generally leading small patrols. You were a Second Lieutenant serving in the counties of Armagh and County Down, is that correct? "You seem to be reliably informed, Sergeant. Please commence."

"On one particular patrol dated 20th of November 1973, your five-man patrol that you were commanding, consisted of Lance Corporal Leonard Sanderson, Privates Derrick Astley, Russell Wilkins, and Jack Stevens. Is that correct, sir?"

"Good God man, how do you expect me to remember a patrol from the many I've been on? anyhow, what's a patrol got to do with my life being in danger?"

"I'm coming to that, sir, now recently a body was found in a lake near Dromore. It was discovered by some boys swimming and that discovery has set off a series of events.

Starting off with the attempted murder of Derrick Astley. He was shot at point blank range, and he is still very poorly, but recovering in a safe location.

Now, only one day ago, Jack Stevens was murdered at his home and Russell Wilkins has been put into protective custody for the moment."

"Do you think they are coming after me, Sergeant?"

"Before I carry on, I'm surprised you didn't ask me about L/Cpl Sanderson?"

"Where is he, is he safe too?"

"Well, sir, when was the last time you saw Leonard Sanderson?"

The Colonel went silent. Tell the truth or lie. The body language of the detective, who was now looking directly into his eyes, convinced him that the detective knew the answer. "I actually met up with Lennie for a drink in a pub. Just for old time's sake a few years ago. He contacted me so I went along, to see how he was getting on."

"A bit unusual, an officer of a high rank, such as yourself meeting up with a junior NCO?" "What you don't understand, Sergeant, is the army is like a family. We look out for one another: there's a bond between the military that exists, which you don't find with civilians."

"You are absolutely right, sir, I couldn't agree more and that's why I'm surprised, when after all these years, you walked into the pub, sat down, spoke to Lennie and didn't order a drink, not even for your old comrade, then got up and left. Can you explain that?" The Colonel was floundering like a fly in a spider's web.

"It wasn't Lennie. A lot of years had passed, and I didn't recognise him. I must have walked into the wrong pub."

"In that case why did you give him an envelope marked *On Her Majesty's Service* to this stranger?"

"I feel I've been ambushed with this, Sergeant."

"Come on, he was black mailing you, wasn't he? And when Lennie left the pub after his final drink, he was promptly run over and killed."

"What, my god, I didn't know that!"

"By the way, the money was taken by the driver."

The Colonel was again silent, like a chess player considering their next move. "How did the killer know I was meeting Sanderson?"

"Bugged more than likely, probably the phone at his pub. People are being murdered, sir, and my job is to stop it and find out what's going on.

There are two possible answers. Someone is employing hit men to liquidate the patrol. If that someone is yourself, then you have nothing to worry about, except people will be asking lots of questions. If you are totally innocent, then you will have to go into hiding like the others.

I am sorry this has been unpleasant for you. Perhaps talk to your lawyer or family as I am now returning to Belfast. I urge you to contact me if anything comes to mind.

Personally, I don't think you murdered anyone, but I know you carry a burden that haunts you, and Lennie Sanderson was exploiting that burden.

I will make my own way out. Goodbye, sir."

The Colonel sat at his desk completely dejected. What was he going to do? The detective was right about the burden he was carrying. He decided to go to the family home and talk to his parents about a good lawyer.

Bristol 23rd July 2002

"How long have we got to stay here in this ... this prison?"

"It's not that bad. We have all the amenities we need, Ann."

"No, Russell, there's nothing wrong with the house, it's missing my parents and the kids, shopping, and my art classes."

"The inspector will be here shortly, maybe he can give us an idea. I'll put the kettle on." Russell left his seat and grabbed the kettle, filled it and continued making two mugs of tea.

Just a few streets away, Detective Inspector Ray Evans was at the wheel of the car talking to his Detective Sergeant.

They were based in Bristol, but today they were interviewing Russell Wilkins in a safe house in Western-Super-Mare. "I don't think they know anything about the death of Jack Stevens yet. Should they be told, sir?" asked his DS.

"Scotty, we're in the car, call me Ray. How long have we known each other?" replied Ray Evans in a very strong West Country accent.

DI Evans was approaching sixty and retirement. He was very overweight and had ignored pleas from his wife and doctor to cut down his weight, but a very popular DI at the station.

"Okay, Raymond," came a sarcastic reply, bringing out a large smile on the DI's face.

"I know where you are coming from Scotty. If we tell them about Stevens's demise, it will give them sleepless nights, and they will be more understanding why we are keeping them safe. If we don't say anything about it, they, or one of them, might get itchy feet and go walkies.

What we know about this assassin is that he is callous, and very intelligent, rumoured to be a former SAS man."

The unmarked police car pulled up outside the safe house, and the two detectives left the vehicle and proceeded to the front door.

"Come in, the kettle's already on," welcomed Ann Wilkins.

They were later all seated with cups of tea, and biscuits at the request of Detective Ray Evans.

Then, he finally decided to break the ice, with the all-important question. "Russell, we need you to give us a full account of what happened on the 20th of November 1973 regarding the patrol. You are an important witness, Russell; we need to take a statement from you," emphasised DI Evans.

"I can't do it sorry, I gave my word, we all did," explained Russell.

"Except one, who refused to take the money.''

"Look, Russell, two of the patrol are now dead, another is seriously ill in hospital, regardless of swearing allegiance to your buddies. Mrs Wilkins, can't you make him see that it's all for the best?"

"Sorry, inspector, I've tried," replied Ann Wilkins.

"Well, you're safe here for now, but I'm afraid it won't be forever. We'd better get back to the station. Thank you for the tea, and Russell, please think about it hard and call me."

Not for the first time the Detective Inspector had failed to come away with a statement from Russell Wilkins, which was a pity, as Rab Anderson turned off the M5 onto the A371 heading to Western-Super-Mare.

Belfast 24th July 2002

"Call for you, Sarge from the scuba team at the lake."
"Thank you, Jenny, I'll pick it up in my office. DS Connelly here."
"Morning, Sergeant, Constable Webb here."
"Constable Webb of the frogman team. I've heard it all now."
"I get the piss taken out of me all the time, Sarge; it's like a 'Carry-On film', anyway, we've got something out of the lake that you will be very interested in."
"Go on, Constable, I'm in suspense here."
"We have a rifle, but it's no ordinary one. It's corroded but the lads reckon it's a sniper's rifle."
"Well done, thank the lads for me. Bag it and let ballistics have a look."
"Just one more thing, Sarge, before you go. It might be totally irrelevant, but there was a motorbike and a helmet near it, which seems odd to us, because there wasn't anything else down there except weeds."
"Thanks for that, Constable, a helmet then also," Pat thought for a moment, "That's very interesting, so bag the helmet as well, and nice work lads, bye." DS Connelly replaced the phone, now deep in thought.

Later in the day, ballistics confirmed that the weapon was a M21 sniper rifle. The DS thought it was time now to have a good chat with Detective Inspector James Walsh.

"Hi, Pat, you're here there and everywhere now. I've hardly seen you."

"Neither has the wife. The case I'm on has given her the grumps a bit. I'm now trying to put things together, sir. It's been like a huge jigsaw, with just a couple of pieces missing… nineteen-seventy-three, five troops go on patrol in the middle of nowhere. A man is shot, mistaken for a terrorist, but no weapon is found, so it's covered up.

We find a body, and now a M21 snipers rifle years later, with a bike helmet at the bottom of a lake. Conclusion … another man was there, saw everything and threw the rifle and helmet in the lake. So, a patrol stumbles on two men, hiding with a sniper's rifle, that arrived there by motor bike at some time. The big question, were they there to make a hit on someone? They were very close to a main road. The patrol may have unknowingly saved an important VIPs life."

"You put all that together, Pat, out of mid-air?"

"It's a theory, Guv, nothing more, but I would be more than happy to hear another one."

"Let's suppose you're right. We need everyone to go over newspapers in the library and find out who and what was happening around that time."

"I agree, Guv, it makes sense,"

"I'm impressed, Pat. Well, done." The praise from DI James Walsh came a bit out of the blue, but Pat appreciated it. "Tea, sir? I'm just about to have one."

"That would be nice, Pat, cheers and I'll get my pipe."

The DS went back to the main office, there was no WPC to be seen, so he made his way to the small kitchen area.

Approaching, he could make out some whispering, so he remained still and tried hard to listen. It was a voice of a female on a phone. He could make out the words 'sniper rifle' and 'ballistics'. Then it went quiet.

He moved forward as WPC Corbett came from the kitchen area. "WPC Corbett, who are you talking to?" Her legs went from beneath her then she suddenly burst into tears.

"It's nothing, Sarge, just a row with my boyfriend. I know I shouldn't use my phone at work"

"Your boyfriend has an interest in ballistics and sniper rifles then. What's going on?"

"I'm sorry, so sorry I had to do it," she blubbed.

"Come with me now to the Inspectors office." In the office WPC Corbett was given the opportunity to explain her actions.

"It was when the two men came to see you, sir. When they finished talking to you, one went back to London and the other man, James started talking to me. He asked me what time I finished work which was five o' clock and invited me for a drink about eight o'clock. He seemed very nice, and we ended up going for an Italian meal.

We went back to his hotel and had lots of drinks. One thing led to another, if you get my meaning and I stayed the night.

In the morning, he gave me a Nokia mobile phone and said it was a gift. But there was something he wanted me to do. Any new developments regarding the case that you're working on, he said I had to use the phone and inform him straight away without anyone knowing.

If I did that, I could keep the phone, and he would destroy the pictures he had taken of me. I don't want anyone to see the pictures, sir."

The DI gave it some thought. He could clearly see that the young WPC was beside herself. "You were tricked and set up by these two men, Constable Corbett. What they did was detestable.

I wish you had come to me in the first place. You made an error of judgement, but I don't wish to take it any further. You have been blackmailed, and I don't like that.

You can go back to the office but leave the phone with me. I won't answer it, but it could come in useful, we might have to feed him some useless information.

Detective Sergeant looked at the DI and commented "That's why they were ahead of us the bastards. How low can you get!"

"I didn't like him in the first place, Pat. He was covering up for someone. I won't rest till we find this so-called Mr James Hawthorn of the secret service, and I don't care how many toes I tread on; I'll have him bang to rights".

"Too right, Guv."

Back in the office, WPC Jenny Corbett sat quietly in the office. With tears still in her eyes, she hoped that what she just told the two detectives would not come back to haunt her.

She had thrown James to the wolves, casting him as a *blackmailer*. Her career in the police was now wobbling and would James ever forgive her. What happened that evening on the 13th of July didn't exactly match what she told DS Connelly and DI Walsh.

Belfast July 13th, 2002

James Hawthorn and his colleague Peter Thompson left the detective inspector's office. "You can carry on to London ... I have some unfinished business here; I'll explain tomorrow. Have a good trip."

Thompson walked off passing DS Connelly's office, observing what appeared to be an argument between the DS and his DC. He smiled to himself as he passed; it was more of a smirk.

James waited till he had disappeared then moseyed over to a WPC he had clocked earlier. "Hi there, where can I get a cup of tea around here? I'm absolutely gagging ...please."

"No problem, follow me."

"Okay, WPC err?"

"Jenny, Jenny Corbett."

"And I'm James, Jenny."

They both went towards the outer-office door and James pre-empted Jenny's next move and opened the door whilst looking at her with a beaming smile. He was out to impress this young WPC.

Now in a corridor, James continued with his *unfinished business* "Could you recommend a decent Chinese, Indian or Italian restaurant, Jenny?"

"I'm not a lover of Indian food so I can't say, but there's a really good Italian restaurant I know, it's about two miles away."

"Well, how about me booking a table for two this evening at eight with you as my guest; my treat and you can tell me all about Belfast city?"

"Blimey, you don't hang around, do you? ...James Bond by any chance?"

"If Mr Bond was in town, Jenny, I'm sure he would have picked the prettiest girl in Belfast, but now I've beaten him to it ... come on, I'll pick you up at 7:45."

Jenny stood there lost for words at the audacious request of a date from a man she had spoken to for less than a minute. All she knew about him and his colleague was that they were from the security services, and whatever they talked about in the DI's office had ruffled a few feathers. Curiosity was beginning to get the better of her; this handsome cheeky guy might reveal what's going on; plus, a free meal.

"All right, James you smooth talker, the canteen door is the one on the right down at the end of the corridor, I'll see you there in five minutes with my address and name of the restaurant."

A few minutes later, James was now seated at a typical cafe table stirring a mug of tea. He contemplated if his plan in bedding Jenny could possibly work. Persuading her to come out on a date just like that, was a major achievement in itself; however, she was very pretty, and he did like her; *shame*.

Later that evening in *Bella Italia*, they were sat at a small table with a glass of wine each. Having ordered their meals, it was Jenny who asked questions first. "I don't suppose you can give me an inkling to what that was all about today?"

"I thought you'd never ask, Jenny ... I can't talk in here, *walls have ears*, but I'll talk to you later when we leave. I must be extremely careful."

"Where we going to then, *Mr Bond*?"

"Before I take you home, I must call at my hotel and collect something, and it's something for you. While we're there, I can talk to you in confidence," his tone was starting to sound serious. "Many people out there think the sort of job we do is glamorous and yes; like the films ... but it really isn't. It can be very lonely and I'm so, so glad you're here with me tonight, and I'm extremely grateful, Jen, is it okay to call you Jen."

"Sure, some of my friends do it's fine," answered Jenny.

"I'm not married, nor do I have a partner as relationships can be very difficult with my type of work.

When I was a captain in the Coldstream Guards, I managed to keep a girlfriend for a while; however, there was this problem of her being a corporal in the WRACs. I was a commissioned officer, she wasn't. That led to arguments as we had to keep our relationship under-wraps. After the breakup, I transferred to the army intelligence corps and the rest I'm sure you can figure out, Jenny." He said, with a few untruths.

Jenny was buying all this listening intently with a few; 'My gods'; 'Wow'; and 'Never'. The truth was very different. Bedding a major's wife, whilst serving in the guards was a definite no, and there wasn't a corporal, he just made it up.

Jenny talked a bit about her life in Belfast and James learned that she also had relationships that had fizzled out; that was encouraging news for James.

After their meal, small talk and paying the bill, they both left the restaurant, collected the car and James drove to the hotel with his thoughts solely now on his plan.

Jenny was also quiet, her mind swimming with thoughts of will he or won't he. She desperately wanted him to seduce her but didn't want to make it too obvious. 'Sod whatever went on in the office, whatever happens next is far more interesting.' She thought.

Outside his room at the hotel, James calmly unlocked the door and entered. He switched the lights on and threw the key onto the bedside table. Jenny followed him in, closing the door behind her. He turned around and looked straight into her eyes.

He saw this beautiful girl, now with her hair let down to her shoulders, unlike their first meeting at the police station. Her makeup was now far more glamorous complimenting her pink blouse and short burgundy skirt, complete with a coy smile.

"JENNY! ... you are the most gorgeous girl I have ever set eyes on. There, I've said it!"

Immediately Jenny put her arms around him and pressed her lips against his. The kiss seemed to last a full minute as both tongues were entwined moving in circles.

His hand moved to the bottom of her skirt and slowly made its way up her thighs until it reached her stocking tops. "Wow ... stockings!" Jenny broke into laughter. At last, the ice was broken.

"Take off your skirt slowly please, Jenny," he commanded as he kicked off his left shoe, using the toe of his right foot. His eyes firmly fixed on Jenny as she unzipped her skirt at the back.

By the time her skirt dropped to the floor he was now minus his trousers, and pulling his lightweight jumper over his head which was then cast away to the bathroom door.

His eyes once again gazed at Jenny standing in front of him, revealing her lovely legs in hold-up stockings and black-lace panties.

"You are so beautiful, Jenny, I want to savour this moment forever," James whispered as he unbuttoned his shirt which also was cast away, leaving him just in his boxers and black socks.

He then moved to his bedside table and picked up a silver camera. "What'ya doing?" A concerned Jenny asked. "Savouring the moment, don't move, just keep that pose." The camera made a whirring clockwork sound as it was switched on. "Smile", the camera clicked, and he placed the camera down. "Don't worry, it's a digital camera, there's no film, so it doesn't go to Boots for developing. It's just for me for those *lonely nights*." He spoke the last two words slowly.

James now moved back to her and held her close and continued with the kissing. He slowly removed her black panties and slid his hand between her legs. He knew she was aroused as small breaths and moans came from her mouth. She could feel his hardness pressing into her thigh and moved her hand into his boxers grabbing his manhood. "Woo, Jenny, just a second." He broke away; moved to the bedside draw and pulled out a loose unpackaged condom. He turned towards Jenny and dropped his boxers and proceeded to prepare himself.

"My ... my ..." Jenny remarked watching intently, "that's something you don't see every day."

"What's that then?" asked an excited James.

"Me, looking at a handsome guy, unrolling a condom over a huge, hard cock." Jenny was burning inside with a tingling sensation, watching him with tremendous anticipation.

He moved over to the bottomless girl and held her hand as he took her to the bed and continued to undress her till, she was totally naked; stockings being the exception.

She lay down on the bed whilst James regarded her body; pert breasts; the triangle of hair in her groin and those fantastic legs.

He then discovered she was slightly tanned except for her waistline. "You've been on a recent holiday then, topless by the looks of your tan?"

"Yes, two months ago in Spain."

"I'm jealous already ... all those guys on the beach watching you ... topless."

"Yes, but those guys on the beach won't be getting what you're going to get now."

She smiled as she started kissing his body, moving in a downward direction.

The next 40 minutes was pure ecstasy for both as they continued their love making.

Afterwards, James had made them both a drink from the small fridge. They were still naked, and Jennie was lying on the bed; stockings still on. It's now or never. He was agitated slightly as he picked up the camera, knowing what he was about to do could go all pair shaped and ruin everything: but it was the plan. He focused the camera on Jennie and snapped away.

"JAMES!" she protested, "You didn't ask me."

"Sorry, but you might have refused. I want this pic to keep me going because I want to see you again, in other words, I want to be with you, even if it means packing in my crappy job. That brings me to why I was at the station today. I'll tell you, but please keep it to yourself."

James had purposely changed the subject to distract her from the nude pictures and gain her interest with today's secret meeting; as promised.

"A government assassin ... he's the dead man who was discovered in the lake," revealed James, "he was a sniper back in the early 70's. On the night of the shooting, he lay in a hideout waiting for a Sinn Fein politician. This politician was scheduled to be driving along the road for an important meeting, and McGinn was tasked to bump him off. It may have been Adams but don't take that as gospel. Anyway, a night-time army patrol stumbled on his hideout by the lake, and he was shot ... 'Dead-as-a-Dodo'. Now can you understand why some of this mustn't come out, Jen?"

"Oh, my fucking god, so that's why DS Connelly was angry?"

"Not quite, you know more than the detectives now. He was angry because we stopped McGinn's picture being published. They have no idea about the intended target and that's where you can help me,"

"Me! What do mean, help you?"

James went to the dressing table and retrieved a small box. "Here ... this is for you. It's yours to keep, a Nokia phone all primed up ready to use. Any progress regarding this case DS Connelly is working on, find a quiet spot and bring me up to date. My number is the only one on the phone."

Jenny sat there in complete silence contemplating the task she was just asked to do. "I'm not at all comfortable about this, James, and have I been tricked into this; the canteen; the restaurant; the hotel and now a Nokia phone?"

"Of course you haven't. I set my eyes on you as soon as I walked into the office, and I admit the cup of tea act was my way of introducing myself. I want you to help me and my department within MI5 and spare a huge embarrassment for the British government. Will you Jenny? When it's over I'll come back for you, if you'll have me ... I've now fallen in love with you, and I'm trusting you not to share this very sensitive information."

"James, I'll be doing this thing behind my colleagues back. What if they find out what I'm doing?"

"Well, they won't find out from me or the department, it's just between the two of us, Jenny. If they find you with the phone; it's a gift off your new boyfriend; true."

"Will you come back when it's over, promise me?"

"Of course, Jenny, tonight has been wonderful, the best ever, talking of which ..." James moved over on top of Jenny's naked body, "and the nights not quite over," he said gazing into her eyes.

James now wondered to himself how he had been smitten by her. This wasn't supposed to have happened and soon as the job is finished, he will be back for Jenny in Belfast.

He did regret some of his lies, and as for the pictures he took; they're no longer needed for cohesion and leverage; she's doing it willingly for James, but he'll still keep them for the *lonely nights*.

London 24th July 2002

James Hawthorn was worried. He was supposed to keep a lid on this but the whole thing was out of control. It was no use ignoring it, so he picked up the phone.

The phone rang about seven times then a voice answered. "It's James here, sir. I'm a bit concerned about the investigation. Did you know that the M21 has been found? and it won't take them long to put two and two together.

Also, is there any need for Anderson to carry on with his killing spree? The police know the names of the patrol, and one named Astley has talked, so now the police know everything that happened."

The voice on the other end of the phone agreed, and told Hawthorn to bring Rab Anderson back in. "Anyway, they have nothing to link us at all, it's just bad luck that the patrol blundered in and killed McGinn."

The voice on the phone spoke once more. James Hawthorn was shocked. "What! kill Anderson … I suppose it's for the best as he knows too much. All right, leave it to me."

James Hawthorn put the phone down and helped himself to a scotch, then dialled Rab's Nokia mobile phone.

"It's Hawthorn here. I have new instructions for you, and your fee. Meet me on the Birnbeck Pier tomorrow night at 23:00 hrs. The security gates at the front will be open for you.

The pier is now closed to the public, so we won't be disturbed."

One hour later he was already on his way to Western-Super-Mare, complete with a tool holdall. He needed to recce the pier so he could work out the best way Rab would meet his death without being seen.

He knew the pier quite well. He went on a couple of holidays there twelve years ago. It was the only pier in England to link to a small island, all three acres of rocks. It had closed in 1994 to the public, as it was considered too dangerous. It was now fenced off at the pier entrance with access via a middle gate, padlocked.

If it was dangerous in 1994, it would be far more deadly now, and in the dark.

Rab Anderson put the mobile back in his pocket. He knew something was wrong. *A change of plan.* That was unusual. It never happens. He decided that evening to stick to his plan and go to Ann Wilkin's parents' house and observe. Maybe Ann Wilkins would turn up, maybe not, but it was the plan. He did wonder how on earth the intel was so spot on.

There must be a mole somewhere.

Western-Super-Mare 25th July 2002

It was a no show as far as the Ann Wilkin's parents' house was concerned.

About 10 p.m. Rab Anderson managed to get some shut eye in a pub car park in Sand Bay. When awake in the morning, he decided to drive into town, park up and enjoy a hearty breakfast. In the town he would be able to get a wash and brush up, hopefully, and after all that have a look at this pier in the daylight.

At 6 p.m. Rab stood before the Birnbeck pier entrance. The gate stood 20 yards in front of him. He thought why on earth come to a dilapidated place like this? It looks like it will collapse with the next gust of wind.

He moved forward to examine the gate and noticed that the lock was brand new. Why a new lock? Then he remembered what Hawthorn had said about the lock.

"Yes, Hawthorn is already here, and Hawthorn has put this lock on and has the keys. What's he up to?" He decided to move away from the pier and find an observation point and wait for Hawthorn.

Today, he was fortunate to have a Browning 9mm pistol fully loaded, plus another little surprise up his sleeve.

Rab thought about how all this mess had started. He remembered the day back in 1969 when he first met Tom McGinn ... on a rainy day in Carrickfergus.

Tom McGinn Carrickfergus 1969

The rain was pouring down as Rab and James Hawthorn pulled up in a car outside a terraced house in Carrickfergus. Hawthorn grabbed an umbrella, exited the car and immediately opened the umbrella and casually walked up the short path to the door and knocked five times.

Rab was the driver and had no umbrella. He locked the car door and ran up the path and joined his colleague.

The door opened and a man who appeared to be in his seventies, stood in the doorway. "Yes," he muttered. "Is it possible we can have a word with Tom? Its military business, sir, here's my identity card." Hawthorn flashed his identity card.

"Just a minute, I'll go and get him. You'd better come in out of the rain." The old man shuffled off as Rab and Hawthorn stepped inside.

The smell of stale cigarette smoke hit them hard as they entered the front room. One look at the former white painted door, which was now a dark yellow colour, confirmed that one or both occupants were heavy smokers.

"His accent is strong, I struggled to catch what he said then," Hawthorn whispered to Rab pulling an expression with his nose, showing a reaction to the pungent smell of smoke.

"There's a fair bit of a Southern Irish in the accent that's why," informed Rab.

"Hello there, I'm Tom McGinn, what can I do for you, boys?" There at the door stood a very confident young man with a smile on his face to back it up. James Hawthorn spoke first. "We would like to take a moment of your time, to discuss a proposition to you in the strictest confidence.

My name is James Hawthorn of the security services, and my colleague is former SAS trooper, Rab Anderson."

"Well, I'm all ears' gents, come with me, we had better go into the back room. It's just through that door there while I'll go and tell the old man that we don't want to be disturbed."

Within a few seconds Tom McGinn entered the room and closed the door behind him. He beckoned the two men to sit and make themselves comfortable.

It was Rab who spoke next. "Before we go any further, Tom, we need your assurance that what we discuss now goes no further than these four walls. I don't need to remind you that as a serving soldier you have already signed the official secrets act. So, not a word to your army mates and say nothing when you've had a few drinks; and most of all, nothing to your family.

If the proposition is not for you, then you can carry on with your normal army life and you will never see us again. Would you now like James to tell you all about it, Tom?"

"I'm intrigued, how can I not hear what it's all about. So, boys, let's hear what you've got to say," replied a very interested Tom McGinn.

"It's a ten-year contract. You will be given your own home, a maximum of three bedrooms and garage, on the mainland. After ten years, it becomes yours for life. You can stay there or sell; it's up to you. You will have access to the very latest weapons, particularly sniper rifles.

Which brings me to the point of why we have picked you. From what we know about you. You are undoubtedly one of the finest marksmen in the UK, and security cleared. That is why we need you.

I have my own department in MI5 and have a free reign over what I deem to be a severe security risk in our country. I am not answerable to politicians or the courts; I work under the radar. In other words, we don't exist. My department is used as the last resort.

If you are interested in joining us, you will be given a new name, and as well as the house, you will receive an income of £20,000 a year. There will occasionally be tax free bonuses for certain jobs.

On a day-to-day basis you will be an armourer, responsible for maintaining and booking out weapons.

There is a downside. You will have to say goodbye to your father for the duration. We are happy enough for you to send him money, but it must be from an overseas bank account though in your new name. You can tell him that you are being posted overseas for security work, and he must not tell a soul.

There are a few minor details that I don't need to go through now. Any questions, Tom?"

"Basically, you want me to be a hit man?" Rab and Hawthorn's eyes both met as they looked at each other.

"Er, yes, if you want to put it like that," replied Rab.

"It's the scum of the earth we're after, Tom, not your average joy driver. Those who escape justice because they have fat cat lawyers and laugh at the law," jumped in Hawthorn who was beginning to sound like a double-glazing salesman. Tom McGinn was still silent, deep in thought about what he had just learned. "I sign a contract then for ten years, and what if I want to leave?"

"The question you should be asking is, 'can I sign another contract after the ten years are up?' do you realise how much money that you'll be making?" said Rab.

"What's your real concern Tom?" asked Hawthorn.

"I have never killed anyone. I know that I would have to as a soldier in a war situation. I have no problem with that. This is different and will I know who I am about to kill?" asked a concerned Tom McGinn.

"Not at all. Just keep thinking that the world will be better off without them. Your target could be a child killer or an international drug dealer responsible for hundreds of deaths. Like James said, scum ... it doesn't bother me," replied Rab.

"So, if you've put a few away then, why do you want me?" asked Tom McGinn.

"I might have been in the SAS, but I'll never be as good as marksman as you, Tom. I'd completely balls it up," laughed Rab.

"One condition I have about this?" asked Tom.

"What's that?" asked Hawthorn.

"Don't put me up against my own countrymen, that's south of the border as well. You will have to put that in your contract or its no deal."

"A hit man with morals. I like it," said an impressed Hawthorn. "Okay, Tom, it's a deal and that can go in the contract. Happy now?"

"You have a new hit man lads. Do you want an Irish whisky now?" said Tom McGinn with a large smile.

Arrangements were then made to give Tom McGinn time to tie up loose ends and have a final drink with mates at the pub, not that his mates knew it was a last drink and then spend a last couple of weeks with his father.

Hawthorn told him not to worry about his CO. The CO would be contacted and put in the picture. *The security services have recruited L/Cpl McGinn and it was not to be passed on to anyone under any circumstances.*

They shared a whisky together and went through the smaller details. Most importantly they emphasised to McGinn about keeping his mouth shut, especially after a few drinks down the pub. Although this would be later be put to the test, but they were not going to mention it to Tom McGinn.

***

Hawthorn knew of Tom McGinn's drinking habits. His local pub was within walking distance, a few streets away, roughly half a mile. Like clockwork, Tom McGinn would turn up every Saturday evening without fail, unless he was on duty.

This up-and-coming Saturday Tom McGinn was free, so Hawthorne had arranged for his colleague, Peter Thompson, to have a low-profile drink at the pub, keeping an eye on McGinn, and see that Tom McGinn behaved himself with his mouth.

The very next Saturday, Thompson sat in a car a few doors down the road from the McGinn's house. He had pulled up at 7 p.m. and had the radio on, waiting for Tom McGinn to exit the house.

He didn't have to wait long. At 8.15 p.m. the front door opened and Tom McGinn, wearing a Donkey jacket and flared jeans, trotted off to the pub. Thompson let him go a few yards then left the car and followed him from a fair distance.

Fifteen minutes later Thompson had arrived at the pub. He decided not to dive straight in but leave the group of men to order the drinks first.

Thompson went back to the car and drove it just a few yards from the pub.

When it turned 9.30 p.m. Thompson left the car and entered the pub, he spotted McGinn in the lounge with two other men sat at a table by the window.

He went to the bar to order a drink, giving himself time to pick the best place to observe, and hopefully listen to what they would be talking about.

The lounge was half empty, and Thompson was happy about that, as the noise level would be better. He sat down at a small table near to the three men, and opened up a newspaper he had with him, as it would appear to be more appropriate as he was on his own. He noticed that McGinn's mates had long hair, so they were ninety nine percent likely to be civilians.

The next thirty minutes consisted of read a bit, sup beer, keep listening. He occasionally looked in their direction then one of the men looked at him as if he was checking him out.

Thompson then buried his head back into the newspaper. He turned a page as if he was engrossed in an article and made a fatal mistake of looking up back at the three men. The same man had seen him look up.

Thompson left the table with his glass and went to the bar and ordered another drink. "Did you see that, the bloke who just got up from the table there … I'm sure he's watching us," said one of the long-haired men. "You sure about it?" asked McGinn.

"Wait till he comes back. I won't look at him. See if I'm right?" said the same man. Thompson sat down with his new drink, resisting the temptation at looking at the three. He was feeling very uncomfortable. *Perhaps this wasn't a good idea* had crossed his mind.

Suddenly there was a tap on his shoulder which made him turn quickly. "Change! you forgot your change," said the barmaid who had just served him. "Oh thanks, sorry about that," replied Thompson.

Now all three men were looking in his direction. Thompson saw them looking at him. Finally, one of the longhaired men spoke up "You've got a problem, mate? You're making me feel uncomfortable."

"And me," spoke the other longhaired man.

"Er, no problem, I forgot my change, that's all," Thompson replied.

"Then why are you so interested in us? We've seen you watching us, so I think it's time you finished your drink and pissed off," said the same man.

"I'm not going anywhere yet; I can see that you're trying to intimidate me." Now Tom McGinn chipped in "You have two minutes to finish your drink, or we'll throw you out on to the street. I think that's very fair don't you, lads?"

"Yeah, very fair," said one of the lads.

Two minutes later outside the pub, two women were approaching when the pub door flung open followed by Thompson coming out at high speed, losing his footing and ending sprawled out on the pavement in front of both women. "Are you all right love?" asked one of the women. Thompson said nothing.

McGinn walked out of the pub on his own and helped Thompson up off the floor and at the same time, he whispered in his ear "Tell Mr Bond and Moneypenny that I'm not fucking stupid. I know what you were up to. Have a good night `M`."

Wiltshire 25th July 2002

Lt Colonel Rory Furness asked for his adjutant and RSM to meet him at his office promptly at 11 a.m.
Both were surprised to see the Colonel in civilian attire.
"Morning, gentlemen, step into my office please. I have some problems at home, so I'm afraid I will have to rely on the two of you to hold the fort. Major Thornley who would normally step in is away on a course this week so are you both comfortable about it?"
"No problem, sir," replied the RSM, then the adjutant also chipped in
"I think I will be able to manage, sir."
"Right, good. I'll be off now then." They both saluted the Colonel as he hurried out of the office.
Rory Furness had a long journey in front of him made longer by the infamous M25 motorway. His family home was in Wiltshire, near Warminster. His father located here as it was a good location as Salisbury Plain, well known for military exercises wasn't too far away.
Later that day, now in the countryside, he drove cautiously as he didn't want to drive past the gates to the house. He saw the sign by the gates *Alanbrooke House*.

His father had renamed the house in 1963, the year Viscount Alanbrooke died. He continued to drive about one hundred yards and parked by the garages.

He walked to the front door of the large country house, and the door was opened by a servant. "I saw you walking over, sir, and your father is waiting in the rear lounge."

"Thank you, Thomas," and so Rory Furness walked to the lounge to face the wrath of his father. "Hello, Father," he said sheepishly, moving into the room.

"Have you seen your mother yet?" his father asked.

"Not yet."

"Well, go and see her, and your sister, because we have a lot to talk about."

"Very well then." Lt Colonel Rory Furness left the room as if he was a naughty little boy.

"Hi, mother." Rory stooped and planted a kiss on his mother's cheek.

"Rory my love, I've missed you so much. It's been ages since we have been together."

"I know, ma-ma, but I have been so busy with the battalion. I've missed you all too, and where's sis?"

"She might be in the stables; it's a wonder she doesn't sleep in there. Anyway, cook will be preparing dinner, so you will see her shortly. She never misses dinner."

"Well, I'm going upstairs to clean up, and get changed. I won't be long and then we will have a good chat. I'll just go and say a quick hello to sis."

Sis, Christian name Louise, was a 47-year-old spinster who had spurned many opportunities of marriage, however her first love has always been her horses.

"Found you!" Rory shouted as he pushed the stable door.

"Rory!" She ran over and put her arms around his shoulders and hugged him. "This is an unexpected surprise."

"I'm just off to the bathroom, but I couldn't go upstairs without saying hello to my favourite sister."

"You sod; I'm your only sister," she said laughing.

"You love those four-legged beasts don't you. I always know where to find you sis, anyway, can't stop, but I'll catch you later. I must get washed and brushed up."

"Bye, Rory, see you shortly." Louise carried on attending to the 'four-legged beasts,' with a large smile while Rory made his way back into the house and carried on upstairs without hardly speaking to his father.

His father, Major General Andrew Furness KBE (retired) was still a director of the armaments factory that he had sold ten years ago.

Born in 1920 he followed in his father's footsteps and joined the army as a cadet at Sandhurst. Rory's grandfather had left the army after twelve years and established a small arms business.

The business became successful, particularly with exports so new premises were built and the firm prospered. The business passed down to Rory's father when the old man died in 1965. However, Rory's father didn't want to give up his military career, so he asked his younger brother to manage the firm. He did, and he nearly ran the company into the ground.

In 1968, he paid his brother off and took control, placing a new man in, former army officer Gregory Fraser, who he had served with for several years. Eventually, the business began to stabilise.

Just as business was taking off again, an unexpected problem arose. The new government minister for defence procurement for armaments, was no friend of Rory's father; they were at Charterhouse school together and there was bad blood between them.

It came to a head when Rory's father gave this future minister one hell of a beating. It resulted in his father very nearly being expelled and the bad blood still existed.

Now this minister was going for payback time.

In 1973, the contracts had dried up, much to the pleasure of their competitors. It was turning into a disaster with workers having to be laid off, creating a very difficult period for Rory's father.

One particular day, Gregory was reading his regular newspaper when he came upon an interesting article. After reading it, he paused and didn't read any more. He put the paper down and grabbed a pen and paper.

As a former officer who served with General Andrew Furness, they had built a strong trust between themselves. They became great friends, and the General admired his colleague's brilliant talent for planning.

That day, after reading the article, he devised a brilliant plan, which was outrageous and then put it to General Andrew Furness.

Western-Super-Mare. The pier 25th July 2002

At 10 p.m. it was now dark. The old decrepit Birnbeck pier lies on the edge of the resort of Western-Super-Mare, which is now very quiet with little activity anywhere. It would make a fitting location for any horror film if one was needed.

The silence was disturbed by footsteps slowly walking up to the gate and Rab could make out a shadow by the gate. He heard the gate being unlocked then the gate grating badly, as it was forced open and then again, as it was returned into position. The shadow slowly moved along the pier occasionally pausing. Hawthorn was doing something, but he couldn't see what.

After about a minute, he continued moving a little more, then, came to a halt. Now, no sound or movement at all.

At 10.55 p.m. Rab moved out of his spot, watched a young couple walking by, perhaps returning after a drink, and stepped onto the road behind them, walking in their footsteps. Once again, he was in front of the gates, observing that the lock had been removed. He pushed the gate, and the grating sound filled the air again. He didn't close it as he slowly made his way along the pier.

The Browning was now in his hand, cocked with the safety catch off. He was right not to put much faith in Hawthorn.

"Hawthorn, it's me, I'm here." He spoke clearly but not too loudly.

"Over here, Rab, keep walking you're nearly here, look for the torch beam."

A beam from a small torch swayed from left to right like a metronome. It seemed very automatic and with his eyes following the light, he didn't see the trip wire that Hawthorn had tied up in the darkness.

Too late, as he fell, he rolled onto his shoulder, but still gripping the pistol. He heard the loud crack of a gun as he fell and a sharp pain in his upper arm. Rab hit the floor and rolled to the right and then there was silence, and both men were looking for movement in the dark.

Rab slowly transferred the Browning to his left hand and put his right hand into his jacket pocket. The pain from his arm was killing him, but he still put every bit of concentration into gently removing the thunder flash from his pocket. With his teeth, he pulled the pin out and threw it a short distance, which landed with a bump and after two seconds; a huge flash and bang.

He saw the silhouette of Hawthorn and without hesitation fired three times at the shape, which was followed by a thud. Hawthorn landed on the wooden decking.

Rab moved over to the body and looked for the torch but couldn't locate it. There was string around Hawthorn's wrist, so he pulled it hard, and something snapped but Rab continued to pull, and the torch landed in his hand. "The crafty bastard," Rab muttered.

Not only had Hawthorn laid a trip wire, but he had also rigged the torch up in the air and pulled the string, causing it to sway. Misdirection, Rab thought, as he carried on searching Hawthorn's pockets. "Phone, I'll have that," he said wincing with the pain, "now, time to go." He made his way off the pier as carefully as possible however, in the distance he heard a voice shouting, "Call the police, someone's got a gun."

"Now ... I have a score to settle with the treacherous shit who set this up, and I know where you live." Rab said out loud.

***

Detective Inspector Ray Evans had just pulled the sheets over him when the phone rang. "Hello, Ray Evans speaking,"
"Sir, its Sergeant Morris speaking from Birnbeck pier. There's been a shooting, and we have a body of a man on the pier."
"I'm on my way, carry on, you know what to do."
By the time the DI arrived, the pier was a hive of activity. More spotlights were being erected, and tape was flapping in the breeze. Uniformed police were searching for evidence with torches.
"Blood over here, sir," one of the uniformed police shouted out.
"Three gunshot wounds to the body, and it looks like one hit his heart," said the forensic doctor who had arrived quickly to the scene. "Do we know who he is, Sergeant?" asked the DI.
"Not yet, sir, but we have taken pictures of the body... shall I search his pockets now?"
"Carry on."
"Driving licence, sir," the sergeant passed it by holding it by the edges.
"James, Hawthorn," the detective inspector read it out slowly, and then gave out his instructions. "I want this place going over with a tooth comb, and it looks like the other man was hit as well. I'll carry on in the morning with this as I need a decent night's sleep for now, Sergeant."
"Goodnight, sir."

26th July Belfast 2002

The phone was ringing out but no one in the office was answering. Eventually DI James Walsh picked up the phone.
"Hello, Detective Inspector James Walsh speaking."
"Good morning, it's DI Ray Evans here from Somerset. It's all been kicking off here.
Last night there was a shoot-out at Birnbeck pier, and we think it could be part of our combined investigation. A body was found late last night on the pier with three bullet wounds in his upper body and we have identified him as, James Hawthorn. We found his driving licence."
"Sorry to interrupt you, but that name sounds familiar, just one second ... Pat!" he bellowed at full volume, "Here quickly." DS Connelly scurried in.
"Guv."
"James Hawthorn, is that the man from security services who ... well you know what?"
"Yes, that's him, I won't forget that name."
"Dead." DI Walsh whispered but then continued with the phone call.
The DS decided to stay.
"Yes, we've had dealings with him not too long ago. He claimed to be from the security services, and he had ID, we checked. We were about to give the go ahead for the press to

publish an older picture of Tom McGinn, who was pulled out of the lake. This is what set off the investigation in the first place. But this Hawthorn fellow threatened us with a D notice.

It's irrelevant anyway, now we know the body was Tom McGinn."

DI Evans continued the conversation. "Well, whoever shot Hawthorn, was also shot, and managed to get away. Western-Super-Mare hasn't had this much excitement since Laurel and Hardy came to judge a beauty contest.

A thunder flash was even used last night. The pier was locked as it's unsafe, but bolt cutters were used to break in.

All hospitals and medical practices have been informed about our wounded fugitive, and roadblocks have been set up on all roads leaving the town."

"Seems like you have it all under control, but I must sign off now as my DS is signalling me frantically. I'll keep in touch."

"What's with all the gestures, Pat?"

"It's just come to me. We have his phone."

"Whose phone?"

"Hawthorn's. We took it off Jennie, didn't we? Hang on, it's in my desk." DS Connelly returned in seconds.

"Hawthorn's number will be on here because Jennie was feeding him information. There is a remote chance the wounded man has nicked the phone. I can but try."

"Very remote would be an understatement," the DI chipped in.

"It's ringing!" The phone rang out a good ten times and the DS decided that the phone must be lying on the pier floor somewhere, suddenly. "Hello, hello, who's this?"

"Is that you Rab?" guessed the detective.

"Yes, who is it? Is it you, Boss?"

"Where's Hawthorn, and why you've got his phone?"

"Hawthorn's dead, he tried to kill me. He asked me to meet him on the pier last night and not long ago he pulled a gun on me and shot me in the arm, but I managed to get away, the pains fucking terrible."

"Okay, where are you now?"

"Just got on to the A372."

"Ring me when you're ten minutes away." DS Connelly put the Nokia down on the desk.

"Right, sir, we're in business, can I have your phone?"

"What you up to, Pat?"

"DI Evans, I'm letting him know that Rab Anderson, the wounded fugitive is heading east on the A372… DC Brookes?"

"Sarge."

"Find out where Colonel Furness is at this moment. Ring his barracks and I'm ringing DI Evans again."

DI Evans answered the phone. "DI Evans, this is DS Connelly. The man you are looking for; his name is Rab Anderson and he's travelling east on the A372. He has a gunshot wound to the arm, but we have no vehicle description, destination unknown. Sorry, sir I must go."

DI Evans was left speechless, sitting at his desk as he replaced his phone. Then he went into overdrive as he called his team together and designated each one their tasks ASAP.

"DC Brookes, any luck?"

"Still trying, Sarge."

"Keep at it."

The DS picked up the conversation with DI Walsh. "I was really lucky, a lucky guess that it was Rab Anderson. Even more lucky is the fact that he thinks I'm 'The Boss'. I couldn't push it any further. Had I asked how long it will take, Anderson could have smelt a rat but now, DI Evans has a better chance if he is considering setting up roadblocks.

If Anderson does ring back, we can calculate roughly where he is heading. Suppose his average speed is fifty miles per hour from the moment he got on the A372. That was about fifteen minutes ago, where would he be roughly?"

"Get me a map, Pat, this is a job for me, it's about time I contributed something."

The DI laid out a map of the UK over the desk, knocking off the pile of papers and his cherished pipe, which irritated him. Then a constable knocked the office door and offered DI Walsh an AA book of maps.

"Err, thank you, Constable. Right, Wincanton A303 or the A37 south of Yeovil, either of those!" The DI cried out in triumph, "well it's my best rough guess." Suddenly, a shout from DC Brookes filled the air, "Warminster!"

"A303 then," remarked DI Walsh.

"Sir, Colonel Furness is at his parent's home near Warminster and I've got the full address. I've just spoke to his adjutant."

"I had this all wrong. I discounted Colonel Furness and now, here we have Rab Anderson heading in his direction," said a shocked DS Connelly.

The DS immediately picked up the phone to update DI Evans and the engaged tone was all he heard. "Come on, come on ... get off the bleedin' line ... engaged, Gov." He persevered with frustration.

26th July 2002 A303 near Warminster

Rab Anderson was in a lot of pain as he struggled to control the vehicle. At one point he nearly collapsed with his foot pressed hard on the accelerator, and overtaking where possible.

There were a few near misses with oncoming traffic. Then finally at last, the junction where he has to turn left onto the A350 to Warminster, and Rab was almost there.

Belfast 26th July 2002

DS Connelly frantically kept dialling the number then banged the receiver down yet again. Suddenly, the ringing tone. "DI Ev ..." DS Connelly cut in.

"Warminster, Alanbrooke House, it's a driveway off the A350." Then the ring tone of the Nokia came into action on the desk. "Quiet everyone," DS Connelly gestured for silence as he picked up the phone. "Yes?" asked the DS.

"Five minutes." said the strained voice of Rab Anderson.

"Okay." DS Connelly switched the Nokia off, and then immediately picked up the other phone. "DI Evans, he's five minutes away."

The phone went dead as DI Evans slammed it down and barked out the address and implored his team of the urgency to act quickly.

Alanbrooke House 26th July 2002

"When will he be here?" asked Rory.

"Gregory will be here shortly, Rory," replied his father. The drawing room was a testament to Major General Furness's military career with pictures of all the different units he served with.

One picture stood out, a group picture with King George taking centre stage; a display of trophies he won playing rugby and paintings from the Far East.

A very large shield with two spears either side was bought back from Nanyuki in Kenya, which was a camp area, used for jungle warfare training for British troops; wood carvings of African animals completed the display.

In the corner of the room, a glass cabinet, locked with two muskets. One oddity was a sign he picked up in Berlin *You are now leaving the British sector*.

"Is Gregory the reason why we didn't have this conversation yesterday?"

"Very much so, Rory. Ah! talk of the Devil." Gregory was brought in by the servant, who then served drinks.

Andrew Furness made himself comfortable in an armchair whilst Rory and Gregory remained standing. Andrew addressed the servant, "I do not want to be disturbed under any circumstances, Thomas. Would you please inform my wife and daughter."

"Understood, sir." The servant left the room and gently closed the door.

"Rory, I'm glad you're here, and that's why I have invited Gregory here today. We have something to tell you. We know you are in trouble so let's turn the clock back to how it all started. Let's go back to your 1973 tour of Northern Ireland. The 20th of November to be precise. You commanded a patrol and later that evening, and you made a mistake."

Rory butted in

"How on earth do you know about that?"

"Quiet, Rory, listen and all will be explained ... let me continue. You saw the shadow of a figure in the dark and assumed straight away that it was a terrorist, and without hesitation you fired one shot and killed him. That would have been fine in a different scenario, but this is Northern Ireland. It was a mistake, but instead of owning up you decided to bribe the patrol.

That must have been with the money that you had off me for this fantastic new car; which I never did get to see. I already knew it was for the patrol and not a car... you were confident that the secret was safe, and it was for a while, until Lennie Sanderson blackmailed you. An arranged meeting didn't go to well on the 6th of October 1998.Peartree pub in Frimley, wasn't it?"

"I didn't kill him, no way."

"I know you didn't, Rory. You are totally innocent, and once again, it was looking like all your worries were over. After all, you were rising in the ranks.

Then the body in the lake was discovered by boys, having a summers dip. The body of Tom McGinn, a former soldier, and a brilliant marksman, and now the investigations by the police are beginning to make progress. You have been interviewed by a Detective Sergeant Connelly."

"How do you know all this? What the hell is going on here?" a very confused Rory retorted. The General continued, "You still haven't worked it out yet." General Furness then let out at full blast. "Tom McGinn was working for me! ... and you buggered up an operation that Gregory had planned with me."

"What ... I don't understand, what operation?"

"You stumbled on a two-man operation. After you killed McGinn, the other operative watched you, and your patrol. He saw the body of McGinn being dumped in the lake. When the ambulance arrived later, Astley ... yes, I know his name, Astley was put in the ambulance and taken to the hospital and the operative followed on the motorbike.

Just like that, we had the information about the patrol. Although you ruined our operation, I have been watching your back all these years since, after all, you are my son ... anyway, Lennie had to go. He was a blackmailer."

"You killed Lennie?"

"Well, not me personally, my operative, who saw you shoot McGinn. He's responsible for the unpleasant business. Astley was next but it was a botched-up job thanks to that Neanderthal McAlister, and Astley survived. Stevens didn't, as the operative saw to that."

"I can't believe what I'm hearing, it's like a bad dream. No wonder you wanted my mother out of the way."

"Stop right there, Rory." His father rose from the chair as he continued speaking.

"You have had a privileged life, everything you asked for, and I made that happen and your grandfather also.

All was going well with the factory when out of the blue, a problem arose. As you well know, we rely on government contracts and so on. A new junior minister is appointed and of all coincidences, this person is a former pupil of Charterhouse school. He detests me because we had a set to at school and I whooped him. He isn't going to renew any contracts so our rivals will have them instead.

Gregory reading the Telegraph, discovers that this minister will be travelling to Northern Ireland on a factory visit. We knew the road and the date.

In England you wouldn't do it but over there ... a very different situation. If a minister is gunned down, who gets blamed? The IRA of course, or a splinter group.

The operation you stumbled upon was set up to do just this. A top sniper and a former SAS trooper, and you took out the sniper."

"I just can't come to terms with this. You, a Major General, now an assassin? It makes no sense."

"Well, we didn't kill him, did we? At the end of the day, it would have been all for nothing as he was involved in a scandal and dismissed from his post.

Rory, when I call it a day or depart from this world, the factory is yours. Gregory and I

ha ..." Andrew's conversation was broken by the sound of the door opening.

"What are you doing here you're sup ..."

"Supposed to be dead you mean? Nobody move, stay still."

Rab Anderson stood there looking very ragged, with a large red patch covering his arms and hands as congealed blood soaked into his clothes. The gun was very real, pointing at all three men. They stood very still. "Why are you here, Anderson?" Andrew Furness demanded.

"Why did you send Hawthorn to kill me you bastard?"

"I didn't and it's nothing to do with me." replied the General.

While the two of them were talking, Gregory noticed that Anderson was flagging. There was only about six feet between them and Gregory thought if he flagged a bit more, and looked in the General's direction, he could rush Anderson, grab the gun and overpower him.

He stood there watching his eyes. Anderson continued his rant. "It's everything to do with you. You employed me to kill for you, and Hawthorn tried to kill me, so I would be out of the way ... one less loose end ... who was going to finish Hawthorn off, Gregory?"

Just as General Furness was about to speak, Gregory rushed Anderson, but Anderson had noticed the movement and fired a single shot from the gun. Gregory keeled over on to the floor as the round hit him in the stomach. "Stay still!" Anderson shouted as the crack of the sound was ringing in all their ears. Gregory was groaning in pain on the floor. "He needs to go to hospital now." cried Rory.

"Ah! says the Rupert (slang for junior officer) who shot McGinn and dumped him in a lake; who paid off his men to cover it up. It was me who saw you do it, old boy." Rory was incensed.

"You are just a cold-blooded murderer," replied Rory.

"Right, General, before you get the bullet. Why did you order Hawthorn to bump me off? no bullshit, I want to know. Talk."

"Exactly as you say, loose ends. I'm a wealthy man, and you would have wanted some of that wealth. Now you know ... no bull shit."

There was a sudden bang as the door flew open, pushed by Rory's sister. Rory grabbed a spear from the display on the wall and threw it hard at Anderson, who like the others had all looked in the direction of the bang.

The spear went through Anderson's body and the tip protruded out of his back. As he started to keel, Rab Anderson pulled the trigger and General Furness went down. Rory's sister let off a piercing scream "Daddy! Daddy! Rory, do something!"

Outside, police cars had arrived with the officers dispersing from the vehicles. Some went to the rear others banged on the door. The servant Thomas opened the door and shouted "Ambulance, we need an ambulance quickly."

***

An hour later the house was full of activity. An ambulance had taken Gregory to hospital, and a WPC was looking after Rory's mother and sister. The SOCO team were busy in the drawing room taking photographs, collecting evidence and writing on clipboards.

The dead bodies of General Furness and Rab Anderson were being prepared for removal when DI Ray Evans had finally arrived. The detective inspector was overwhelmed with the horrific sight before him, as he noticed officers with Rory Furness, now clasped in handcuffs, being escorted towards a patrol car, in preparation for his transportation to the station at Bristol.

Statements were taken from his mother, sister and the servant.

Later at the station, DI Evans phoned DI James Walsh in Belfast, and DI George Lane at Wolverhampton police station to bring them up to date regarding the consequences of the shootings.

Bristol 26th July 2002

"Mrs Wilkins, Detective Inspector Ray Evans here."
"Afternoon, Inspector."
"Good news, Mrs Wilkins, you can go home. It's over now, you and your family are safe."
"Russell quick, sorry, Inspector. I've just called my husband, what's happened then?"
"There has been a serious incident resulting in three deaths. I am not prepared to say any more than that at this stage. The important thing is now you can go home."
"Thank you for letting us know, Inspector, goodbye." She turned to Russell and put her arms around him, "Oh, Russell, it's all over."

Wolverhampton 26th July 2002

DI George Lane knocked the front door of Mary Astley's home. "George. How come you're here? What's happened?"

"Really good news, Mrs Astley. There's nothing more to worry about. I've just received a call from my opposite number in Bristol. There has been a major incident down there, and I don't know all the facts, but suffice to say, you're safe and no more walking to the hospital again every day."

"Tell me, George, where is my husband. I'm dying to see him?"

"You know what, Mrs Astley. I've been waiting to tell you this for the last four days. You will laugh your socks off when I tell you."

"For God's sake, George, tell me, you're killing me."

"Well, here we go then. The maternity ward at New Cross."

"NEVER! Oh my God, he'll never live this down. George ... you are right, I will laugh my socks off." DI Lane continued.

"He will soon be moved back to his old ward, then you can go and see him, and I think he'll have a big smile on his face when he sees you."

"Thank you, George, for everything. I'll be eternally grateful for your help."

"Goodbye then, Mrs Astley." George left, still chuckling about the maternity ward.

Belfast 26th July 2002

Detective Inspector James Walsh called for everyone to assemble in the main office.

"Alright everyone, quiet now as I have some news for you." Immediately there was a hush as DI James Walsh spoke.

"I have just received a call from DI Ray Evans in Bristol. Thanks to all your hard work and tenacity, I am pleased to announce the end of the current investigation, well very nearly.

Hawthorn, one of the so-called security officers who gave us a visit, and wound everyone up, was found dead on a pier in Western-Super-Mare in a strange turn around in events. He went there to kill the man we've been trying to locate."

No one in the room had noticed the look of horror on WPC Jenny Corbett's face when Hawthorn's death was announced; all eyes were on DI Walsh.

"However, he didn't succeed, and he became the victim, and from what we are learning about Hawthorn, it appears that he had his own agenda within the security services. While he was a security officer, he was also tied up with Major General Furness, the father of Lt Colonel Rory Furness.

As for Rab Anderson. He made a mistake by taking Hawthorn's Nokia mobile phone and DS Pat Connelly had the incredible audacity, to phone the killer for information impersonating the man behind the operation. We were very lucky to have in our possession Hawthorn's other mobile."

He looked at WPC Jenny Corbett, as if to acknowledge her help with the existence of the other phone, but to his disappointment she had her head bowed down. He never noticed the tears that had welled up in her now, red eyes. He composed himself quickly, "how the killer did not pick up a Belfast accent ... that's one for the bloody history books."

After a few laughs he carried on. "Unfortunately, there were deaths, and one of the deceased is the killer. That information, by the way, is off the record for the time being.

What started as a body being discovered in a lake after twenty-nine years, opened up a can of worms of huge proportions, and now we have the man responsible for that killing, in custody with the Bristol police.

He will now be questioned later by DI Evans and his team. So, a big thanks to you all of you, and I'll see you for a pint at the 'Green Man' after work." Everyone gave a cheer and some clapped. ... but not Jennie Corbett.

Bristol 27th July 2002

DI Evans and his DS were having a final word before the interview with Colonel Rory Furness. He was already with his solicitor in the interview room. He had been cautioned and arrested the previous day.

"Ready, Scotty?"

"Aye aye, sir," an in joke between them.

"Let's go," replied DI Evans.

They joined the two men in the interview room. DI Evans pressed the record button on the tape machine and formally introduced themselves.

The solicitor spoke first. "My client, Colonel Rory Furness has prepared a statement that he would like to read, is that acceptable to you, Detective Inspector Evans?"

"Please carry on, I will call a halt if for any reason I'm not comfortable with it." The solicitor beckoned his client to read the statement.

"I, Lieutenant Colonel Rory Furness, will read an account of events relevant to my involvement of the death of Mr Tom McGinn, and my following action. I do this to save police and the prosecution service valuable time.

I was responsible for the death of the man we now know as Tom McGinn. I took the decision to fire my SLR rifle at an unknown figure I saw in darkness, I could only make it out as a shadow which I took it as a threat. Working in a hostile environment in Northern Ireland 1973, the lives of myself, and the men in the patrol were paramount, and I had to make a split-second decision, as the shadow I saw was rising to a kneeling position, as if to fire a weapon. I fired one single shot then moved forward. Later, when I realised that my men and I could not find a weapon, I was mortified, that it appeared that I had killed an innocent man. Some might say, under the circumstances I was right, others wrong.

I certainly didn't set out that day to kill a man. I then, with retrospect, made a very bad decision. Covering up my action, by offering money to the men of the patrol. In other words, buying their silence. It was my idea not theirs, and it was my decision to dispose of the body by putting it in the lake. My military career is over now, so I am willing to cooperate with the police.

As for my father's actions and his accomplices, I deny any knowledge of what their intentions were. The 26th of July, yesterday, was the first time any of this came to light. I was appalled with my father when he revealed all to me. ... When the man with the gun entered the room, he argued with father, accusing him of ordering Hawthorn to set him up, then, kill him. Gregory was shot by the gunman when he attempted to rush him.

Later, when my sister opened the door, as she would have heard the gun shot, it distracted the gunman, so I took the spear off the wall and threw it at the middle of the gunman's torso, fatefully killing him.

My life is over Inspector; I will cooperate with you. I have to pay for my mistakes ... how is Gregory?"

"He'll live; he's undergoing surgery as we speak.

Thank you for that statement. You have a court appearance this afternoon Mr Furness. The charges will be read out to you, and you will be asked how you plead. The magistrate will then make any decisions.

Your solicitor will go through everything with you Mr Furness. We may still have to ask some questions, but your statement has been very helpful."

DI Evans ended the interview and switched off the tape machine.

Later the solicitor was alone with Rory Furness. "I have now formally been informed by the CPS that you will be charged with perverting the course of justice; for disposing of a body; withholding evidence; and manslaughter for the killing of Mr McGinn.

It's what I expected, although we can argue some exceptional circumstances which you have already included in your statement. You're pleading guilty, so I will be applying for bail.

Right, well I'm in court later today so I will soon find out."

His solicitor stood up and began to place papers into his briefcase, then looked towards his client, "You're taking it very well, Rory, I must say."

"I have had a good run, I'll see you later in court." sighed Rory Furness.

***

In court the charges were read out by the Magistrate and Rory Furness pleaded guilty. His solicitor applied for bail, and it was given subject to conditions Rory Furness had to agree to.

He was to stay in his place of residence, which will now be the family home, attend a police station daily and give up his passport.

The next time he attends court will be for sentencing.

That night, Rory Furness spent his first evening with his mother and sister. He was very fond of them and felt sorry for them for the ordeal they had been through.

The three of them talked for hours, then finally went to their rooms.

***

In the morning, Rory's sister made a cup of tea around 9 a.m. It was late for her as she normally rises about 7.30 a.m. She decided to leave her mother in peace as it was a late night for her. About 9.30 a.m. she made a cup for her brother and took it up to his room.

She knocked the door a couple of times. "Tea, Rory, can I come in?" no answer, "Rory tea," she said louder. She decided to enter his room, but there was no sign of him. She looked at his bed and it clearly hadn't been used.

Then she spotted two envelopes and picked them up; one had her name on and the other her mother's.

Hi Sis, by the time you are reading this I'll be long gone. I always knew that one day my secret, that has been a burden to me, would surface. I made a mistake and as an officer in the British army, a mistake can finish your career. I'm now starting a new chapter in my life, and I feel sure I will find peace. What Father did was incomprehensible and I can't forgive him for what he did. I hope you will forgive me for leaving you in the lurch.

Look after Mother. I will always love you. Your ever-loving brother Rory.

She read it once more as tears rolled down her cheeks. Rory had planned his escape, she was sure. Rory never does anything at a moment's notice. An idiom that sums up Rory and yes, she was convinced that he'd bloody well planned it.

She kept quiet and never said a word about both letters. Two policemen finally turned up and she played dumb. Her mother was no help to the police whatsoever.

"He's absconded, sir," the news was gently broken to DI Evans.

"He's played us all along."

"Shall I inform division, sir?" Scotty piped up.

"Division! What can they bloody well do, he's planned all this.

He fooled us all with that confession, it may be true, but we were taken in.

We'll never see him again ... shit!"

***

The yacht sailed away from Plymouth and there was a fair wind blowing.

Rory stood gazing at the land he will never see again, but it really didn't matter. He had an excellent false passport.

The yacht was fifty percent his, the other half belonged to his partner. A partner since 1975 he could never talk about until the year 2000 because having a male partner in the military was illegal until that date. Even then, *best not mention it old boy.*

"Hi Rory, want another coffee?"

"Please Brandon, only one sugar this time."

***

Three weeks later at a graveside of a church in Carrickfergus, stood the lonely figure of Eamon Dargon.

He was wearing the headdress of 'The Irish Rangers'; the Caubeen. A black jacket with the Irish Rangers emblem on the left; the regimental tie was knotted around the collar of his white shirt.

He stood to attention in front of Tom McGinn's grave and saluted, and paid tribute by calling out the Irish Rangers motto; which translates into *Clear the Way.*

"Goodbye to ye ... old friend, *Faugh A Ballagh*, may you now rest in peace."

Eamon Dargon then slowly walked away with tears in both eyes.

The end.